THE "NO NAME SERIES."

WHAT IS THOUGHT OF THE PLAN.

"The first of the 'No Name Series' of novels is 'Mercy Philbrick's Choice;' and, if its successors nearly approach the excellence of this, the series will speedily have a very wide and favorable name." — *Hartford Courant.*

"The 'No Name Series' of novels is rather a happy idea upon the part of the publishers. Curiosity will naturally stand on tiptoe, eager to discover through the author's style his or her identity." — *Chicago Daily Inter-Ocean.*

"The inauguration of the 'No Name Series' was a happy thought. Nothing adds fascination to a really good literary work like the uncertainty or mystery of its authorship, and the public have read and are reading the new novel with avidity, in order that each constituent member of it may pass judgment. . . . 'Mercy Philbrick's Choice' is a novel that will give the 'No Name Series' an acknowledged place in literature, and stimulate curiosity to meet its successors." — *Boston Post.*

"If the succeeding volumes of the series are as good as this, its success will be assured, and curiosity will run high concerning the authorship of the various volumes." — *New York Independent.*

"The conception of the series is entirely unique. . . . 'Mercy Philbrick's Choice' is a felicitous introduction to just such a series of novels as the one projected, and, if merit shall decide its popularity, an enthusiastic reception may be predicted for the book." — *Hartford Post.*

"It is a good idea." — *Troy Whig.*

"If its successors shall prove to be as good as 'Mercy Philbrick's Choice' is, the fortune of the series is well assured." — *New York Evening Post.*

"The 'No Name Series' promises to be an interesting and piquant literary enterprise." — *Portland Press.*

"The name business in our literature is terribly overdone, and, if the remaining stories of this series are as good and clever and well written as this one is, 'Mercy Philbrick's Choice,' readers will learn to trust more to their own taste and judgment, and rely less on reputations." — *New York Graphic.*

"The typographical appearance of the series is quite tasteful, paper, type, and ink are good, and the page shapely. The cover is black, the title showing in black against a broad red bar; while to avert bad luck and persuade success the cover presents, also in black and red, the four-leaved clover and the ancient horseshoe." — *The New York Christian Union.*

"The story is a very pleasant one, and will make a very favorable impression for the whole series." — *Syracuse Standard.*

"The plan is an exceedingly happy one, — will gradually elevate a discriminating taste and establish a higher standard in fiction." — *Washington Capital.*

"The story is an admirable introduction to the new series, which has for its motto, 'Is the gentleman anonymous? Is he a great unknown?' and appears in a novel and pretty binding of black and red, with ornaments of four-leaved clover and horseshoes." — *Boston Daily Advertiser.*

ROBERTS BROTHERS, PUBLISHERS,
Boston.

NO NAME SERIES.

DEIRDRÈ.

NO NAME SERIES.

"Is the Gentleman anonymous? Is he a Great Unknown?"
Daniel Deronda.

Deirdrè.

BOSTON:
ROBERTS BROTHERS.
1876.

ARGUMENT.

THE King of Eman goes to a banquet in the house of Feilimid, his Story-teller. During the festivity, Deirdrè, the daughter of Feilimid, is born. Caffa prophesies of her future beauty, and of the destruction it will bring on Eman and on the King and nobility. The nobles thereupon demand the death of the infant; but the King orders her to be shut up in a strong place till she grows old enough to become his wife. In course of time, Deirdrè and Naisi, son of Usna, fall in love with one another; and Naisi and his two brothers carry her away to Alba, and take military service under the King. The Albanian King falls in love with Deirdrè, and tries to compass the death of Naisi and his brothers, who escape with Deirdrè to a certain beautiful island in the sea. Thence they are decoyed by the King of Eman, who gives surety for their safety. They return under the guarantee of Fergus, son of Roy; but the King, breaking his oath, has them murdered on the Green of Eman. The lamentations of Deirdrè, and her death.

THE action of this poem begins near Armagh, north of Ireland, in the ancient palace of Emania, wherein dwelt at that time Connor, the renowned and powerful King of Ulster. It then changes northward to the coast opposite Rathlin Island; whence, finding their fleet burnt by the King's troops, the Usnanian princes fly westward, till they arrive at the sound between Tory Island and the mainland, where the galleys of the Fomorian pirates are lying at anchor. There their herald is treacherously slain by Talc, the Fomorian King, and they betake themselves towards the south till they come to the beautiful plain of Irris Domnan, in Mayo, where they accept the hospitality of Keth, the great captain of the troops of Mab and Olild, joint sovereigns of Connaught. Thence they proceed westward to the coast of Irris Domnan, where they slay the Fomorians and capture their fleet, in which they sail away round the northern shores for Alba, or Scotland. Crossing that part of the Atlantic between the Giant's Causeway, Isla, and Alba, anciently called the Sea of Moyle, they sail northward by the coast of Cantyre, and at last take refuge, and build their dun, or town, near Loch Etive, in Argyle. Here they accept military service under the young Albanian King, who, hearing of the exceeding beauty of Deirdrè, falls in love with her. Thereupon the three Usnanian princes, with Deirdrè and their tribe, take refuge in one of the Hebridean Islands; whence after some time they are decoyed by the agents of the King of Ulster. They sail again back to the Irish coast, and land at Beal Farsad, now Belfast; whence they march inland to Emania, where the action of the story ends with the slaughter of themselves and their whole tribe.

CONTENTS.

DEIRDRÈ.

THE FEAST IN THE HOUSE OF FEILIMID.

IT happed in Eman at the joyous time
When wood-flowers bloomed, and roses in their prime
Laughed round the garden, and the new-fledged bird
'Mid the thick leaves its downy winglets stirred,
That the King's Story-teller, Feilimid,
'Mong all the bloom that, like a bright robe, hid
The earth's dark places, felt himself full sad,
He knew not why, and sent, to make him glad,
His henchman with a message to the king,
The nobles and the knights, and all, to bring
From the bright palace straightway to his house,
That they might hold therein a gay carouse.

And the king came, with knights and nobles all,
And soon their shields hung o'er them in the hall:
Buckles were loosened, belts and swords thrown
by,
And pleasure sparkled in each warrior's eye.
Full soon the old man felt his soul restored,
As laugh and jest were bandied round the board,
As the king smiled upon him kind and gay,
As songs were sung, and harps began to play,
And cups were kissed by many a bearded lip,
And care from all hearts loosed its felon grip.
And higher rose the heart-inspiring hum
Of the glad revel through the banquet room,
As the blithe hours went on with laughter meet,
With merry jest and minstrel's music sweet,
And lay of war and tale of maid and man,
And clash of cup and clinking of the can.

Upon that revel gay the sun went down,
And the pale night put on her starry crown;

Yet higher rose the joy and jollity
Of the Great King and all that company:
Till at the very topmost of their mirth,
When jokes and jovial wit had brightest birth,
And all their hearts with generous wine were high,
Through the whole house there rang a mighty cry, —
A long, shrill-sounding, quivering wail of woe,
Like the young heifer's cry in her last throe
When a great snake coils round her on the heath,
Crackling her bones and crushing out her breath.
Round the blithe board the revellers sat still,
As rose again that cry more wild and shrill:
Amazed, some held on high th' untasted cup,
Some at their swords and shields looked furtive
up;
Some, readier of hand, with nervous grip
Clutched the long blade that dangled at the hip,
And eyes sought eyes with quick inquiring glance;
Till Feilimid arose, as from a trance
Of terror, with pale face, —

"O guests!" he said,
"What means this cry of anguish and of dread?
Instinctive in my heart its pangs I feel,
Like the sharp griding of the poisoned steel!
Tell me, O Caffa! — tell! thou great and wise,
Who knowest why morning dawns and daylight dies,
And comets glare and tempests pelt and beat,
And the fierce Thunder-god his brazen feet
Stamps in grim fury shaking earth and sky, —
O wise one, tell what means this woful cry!"

Then Caffa spoke, — the King's own hoary sage,
To whom all Nature like a golden page,
Well conned, lay open, full of wondrous things, —
"O knights and minstrels, — O Great King of kings,
And thou, good friend of mine, O Feilimid, —
From me of Nature's secrets few are hid.
Well do I know this portent, — well I know
Why rings throughout the house this cry of woe:

Thy wife, O Feilimid, in travail lies,
And in his strength some god speaks through her
cries;
And with the last to thee a babe is born,
Bright as the dawn of May's most glorious morn!
Then let the feast go on! The goblets fill,
And round the board a great libation spill
Unto the mighty gods of Earth and Sea,
And Air and Fire, for a good destiny
To the poor babe new-born, though all in vain
I know shall be our prayers!"
Then rose again
The hubbub of the feast, as King and knight
Upstood, and brimming filled the goblets bright,
And raised them with a shout their tall heads
o'er,
And turned them down, till on the shining floor
The wine flowed like the plenteous April rain,
Spattering their long limbs with its ruddy stain
Like the red tide of battle!

Through the hall
The guests again were silent one and all,
As from a far-off door there came a noise
Like that a strong wind makes, which blustering toys
With the wood's leaves upon a summer day ;
And from the door in solemn slow array
A bevy of old beldames, two by two,
Paced rustling up the hall in varied hue
Of shawls and scarfs and robes and broidery
Of silk or serge, befitting their degree
As palace women. First of all there came
Old Lavarcam, the Conversation Dame
Of the Great King, who told him all the sport
And loves and plots and scandals of the Court.
A pace before them walked she mincingly,
And to each great lord bent the pliant knee ;
Sharp eyes she had, each speck and fault that saw,
And face as yellow as an osprey's claw,
And wrinkled, like tough vellum by the heat,
As moved she toward the monarch's golden seat,

Smirking and smiling on the baby bright
That in her arms lay clad in lily white,
With large blue eyes and downy yellow hair,
And skin like pink-leaves when the morns are fair.
With many a bow she stopped before the King,
Then turned to Feilimid:—

"To thee I bring
This babe thy wife gave birth for thee to-night.
Did mortal brain e'er dream so fair a sight?
Did mortal eye since Miled's day behold
Such radiant skin, such hair of downy gold?
No! never on this earth thou'lt find her peer:
Then let great Caffa tell, the noble seer,
If this sweet bud shall grow to woman's bloom,
And what of joy or grief shall be her doom!"

Then Caffa rose, at first with peering gaze,
Like one who looks through morning's misty haze
To see some dark things hid in plains beyond;
Then his eyes flashed: then with light hand and fond

He touched the little babe on brow and breast,
And thus to her alone these words addressed:—

"O lovely little bud of womankind,
In thy short day small gladness shalt thou find,
Though thou shalt bourgeon into bloom and be
Fairest of women! Mighty queens shall see
Thy fame spread wide, fulfilled of envy's gall,
And long for thy destruction. Kings shall fall
Before thee. Each thread of thy yellow hair
For some great hero's heart shall be a snare
Of love's enchantment: blue shall be thine eyes
As the deep sapphire depths of April skies;
White pearls thy teeth, thy lips and bright cheeks red
As berries in the bosky wildwood bred
'Neath summer suns, and fair and smooth thy skin
As the soft satin rose-leaves white and thin
Of the King's garden in the prime of June!—

Alas for thee, that ere the woful noon
Of thy young day, — that day of grief distraught, —
Full many a deed of darkness shall be wrought!
For thou, all beautiful, shalt wake the fire
Of jealous anger and insane desire
In many a hero's heart; and war's red field
Shall gleam with levelled lance and brazen shield
And thirsty sword, where hostile banners rise
Of kings renowned, to win thy smiles and sighs:
Alas! for in thy day, and all for thee,
Great Usna's sons shall die by treachery
And the King's wrath; and from that deed of
shame
Fair Eman's halls shall feed the ravening flame
Of war and carnage, kindled by the light
Of thy destroying glances, till the night
Of woe enwrap the land accurst of men,
O Deirdrè, evil fate beyond our ken!
O leveller of Ulad's fair abodes!
O beautiful bright firebrand of the gods!"

Then rose an aged lord with haughty air
And shaggy brows and grizzled beard and hair,
Whose fierce eye o'er the margin of his shield
Had gazed from war's first ridge on many a field
Unblinking at the foe that on him glared,
And might be ten to one for all he cared.
Now unto all things was he callous grown,
And his hard heart was like the nether stone,
As on the babe he bent his dreadful eye:
"O King!" he said, "O champions great and high!
O minstrels! list this tale I tell to ye
My father brought from lands beyond the sea:—

Far in the North, a smooth Hebridean strand
Spread to the changeful heavens its silvery sand,
And o'er it in a vale 'mid cliffs and rocks
A village gleamed, whose herds and woolly flocks
Fed o'er the inland downs and ferny dells
And breezy moorlands gay with heather bells.

Joyful the village life by shore and mead ;
They reared their flocks and sowed their barley seed,
And fished the fruitful sea when winds were light,
And prayed unto the good gods morn and night,
And sheared and reaped in peace and quietness,
Unknowing envy's pangs or war's distress.

One young June day, when Winter with shrill groans
Felt coming death through all his frozen bones,
And three long days had struggled in the North
In storm to march his drunken army forth
Of icebergs toppling o'er the ocean swell
Against the South from their cold citadel,
A strong wind's voice mixed with the breakers' roar ;
The villagers had gathered by the shore,
To watch the icebergs' terrible array,
Over the waters stretching far away.
Some bright with sun-gleams, some enwrapt in
cloud,
Some struggling each 'gainst each with thunder loud

On their long march to fight the joyous sun,
And in the fight to find themselves undone.
And as the people looked, upon the floe
They saw a little thing as white as snow
Come towards them with the tide the wind before,
Till a great breaker dashed it on the shore.
A small, frail thing it was, with pearly hair, —
The far-sent offspring of the Northern Bear,
And to their simple minds a thing like it
Upon their windy shores had never lit;
As weak it moaned like a young lamb that wails
For its lost mother in the lonesome dales.

Then Erc, a fisherman, fell on his knee
And cried, 'Some god hath sent his progeny
To bless our village and to be our stay
In time of joy, or in the evil day:
So let us build a temple fair and new,
Where we may worship it with reverence due,

And give the heedful god his full content
Of glory for the bright boon he hath sent!'
Straightway they built a temple o'er a spring
That to the wind and sun its waves did fling
Beside the village green with murmuring sound
Of gladness all the changeful seasons round,
Since Mananan, the Sea-god, first upthrew
The wild isle's stony ribs unto the blue.
And there within that temple's fair abode
They worshipped year by year their new-found god,
And morn and eve they fed it daintily
Upon the best fruits of the land and sea,
And morn and eve within the fountain bright
It washed its woolly coat all silvery white;
And as the years went on it grew and grew,
Till the great bull that ranged their pastures through
Seemed like a heifer when it stood a-nigh:
And thus it fared till ten long years went by
In happiness, and to the people brought
Each dream they dreamed, and each fond wish they
sought.

One day of summer, when the village men
Were far away by mountain and by glen
Hunting or herding, or on ocean's field
Fishing for what the teeming waves might yield,
And on the green the children were at play
With merry gambols 'neath the genial ray,—
The mighty she-bear stole from out her house
With step as noiseless as the small brown mouse
Makes when a crumb of bread is on the floor
And the cat nigh, and ranged the bright green o'er
As was her wont.

Beneath a hawthorn-tree
A little child sat weeping piteously,
With a great thorn in his white foot sunk deep
That made the red blood flow. Then 'gan to creep
The great bear round him snuffing, till she came
And licked the blood; then shot a dreadful flame
From the fierce depths of her red rolling eye,
And like a fiend she reared her head on high

O'er the fair child, and with fell face and grim
In hot blood wallowing tore him limb from limb;
Then turned she on the children all around
And slew them, till the smooth green's grassy
ground
Was all one mass of steaming flesh and gore
And echoing to her loud remorseless roar!

Up from the sea-beach in that hour of fear
Old Erc returned, and drave his iron spear
Into the great bear's heart, and slew her. Then,
From the hills running, came the village men;
And Colp, the father of the first slain child,
In his blind ecstasy of vengeance wild
Fell upon gray-haired Erc and took his life:
Then Erc's strong grandson buried deep his knife
In Colp's brave heart: and then in parties two
The people ranged themselves, and slew and slew,
Strong knee to knee and bloody sword to sword;
And the deep vale the echoing terrors roared,

Till the great sun beyond the island hills
Cast his last beams upon the red blood rills,
And the pale moon arose, — when nought was seen
But death and ashes where blithe peace had been! —
What with the she-cub first should they have
done?" —

"Slain it upon the strand!" cried every one!

Then on the babe the warrior looked again,
And sternly said, "Thus let this child be slain,
That we may scape unsuffering from the sting
And gall of the black woe that she shall bring!"

As when, mid Allen's bogs, some sunny day
The wild geese with their offspring are at play,
And as they gambol by the lakelet's edge
The hunter's arrow shears the rustling sedge
And splashes in the shallow marsh thereby;
At once the wild fowl raise their signal cry

Of danger, and loud cackling in their fear
Some hide in reeds, some seek the middle mere,—
So at the grisly warrior's words of doom
The aged dames 'gan rustling round the room;
Some fled the hall, some gathered round the child,
And shrieking clapped their hands with clamor wild.
Then up stood Feilimid, and strove to lull
The tumult; but his heart of pain was full,
And the grief-laden words stuck in his throat:
Then rose the king's voice like a clarion note,
Joyful and speaking gay words full of cheer:—

"O men!" he said, "what marvel do ye fear
In this small baby beautiful and bright?
As well feel terror at the morning's light
That comes as Nature sends it; at the sheen
Of springtide when the fields put on their green;
Or at the lovely leaves and golden flowers
That bloom at summer in bright Eman's bowers!

Be sure the fates no treachery intend,
Be sure the mighty Gods could never send
A thing on earth so beautiful as this
To make our sorrow and to mar our bliss.
Then let us rather thank the Glorious Ones
Who rule in heaven, and roll the stars and
suns,
That they have thought us worthy here below
On our dull lives a treasure to bestow
Of beauty like this babe beyond all price:
Then, cease your fears and let my words suffice,
No harm shall come to Eman in her day,
For I will build a palace fair and gay,
Where she shall blossom like the fairest rose
That in the loveliest bower of Eman blows,
And in the tide of time in Eman's hall
Shall be my bride, the best-belov'd of all!"

Then rang the carven rafters to the shout
The revellers gave; and then the merry rout

Went on once more with tenfold joy and zest,
With minstrel's tale, and jovial song and jest,
Till morn's gay star rose o'er the golden sea,
And sent to slumber all that company.

THE PALACE GARDEN.

NEAR Eman's hall, beyond the outward fosse,
There was a slope all gay with golden moss,
Green grass and lady ferns and daisies white,
And fairy-caps, the wandering bee's delight,
And the wild thyme that scents the upland breeze,
And clumps of hawthorn and fair ashen trees.
And at its foot there spread a little plain
That never seemed to thirst for dew or rain;
For round about it waved a perfumed wood,
And through its midst there ran a crystal flood
With many a murmuring song and elfin shout,
In whose clear pools the crimson-spotted trout
Would turn his tawny side to sun and sky,
Or sparkling upward catch the summer fly;

On whose green banks the iris in its pride,
Flaming in blue and gold, grew side by side
With meadow-sweet and snow-white ladies-gowns,
And daffodils that shook their yellow crowns
In wanton dalliance with each breeze that blew;
And there the birds sang songs for ever new
To those that loved them as friend loveth friend;
And there the cuckoo first his way would wend
From far-off climes and kingdoms year by year,
And rest himself and shout his message clear
Round the glad woods, that winter was no more,
And summer's reign begun from shore to shore.

Beside that merry streamlet all day long,
From month to month, was heard the craftsman's
song:
For they were gathered there from many lands,
And fast the palace grew beneath their hands,
Until each fretted roof and cornice fold
Shone through the woodland sprays like fiery gold.

Then round the flowery slope and level space
They built a giant wall, from cope to base
Unbroken, save by one small massive door
With the king's shield in porphyry fashioned o'er,
And guarded by a triple gate of brass
Through which, unbid, no living wight could
pass.
And never upon mortal's proudest dream
Did such a fairy sight of splendor gleam
As that gay palace glowing in the light,
With door-ways carven of the silver white,
And doors of burnished gold and ivory,
And halls roofed o'er with the pink cedar tree;
And garden glorious with all flowers that grew,
And lawn in whose green midst a jet upflew
Of water from a well of carmogal,
Backward again all diamonded to fall
In breeze-blown mists and showers of glittering
spray
Upon the gold fish at their happy play.—

And there they nursed the babe on breast and knee
Within these palace halls full tenderly;
And there she grew and blossomed year by year
In light and loveliness without a peer,
Like a fair fragrant flower that time by time
Gains some new beauty in its summer prime;
And oft about the garden she would run
And like a fairy dance in shade and sun,
And make companionship with every thing
That through the garden moved on foot or wing.
And scarce seven years had passed till with her tongue
Nimble with elfish questions she had wrung
The very heart from out her nurse's breast:
And all this time did no eye living rest
Upon her, save the king's own royal eye
And Caffa's, and the lady's proud and high
Who nursed her, and old Lavarcam's, the dame,
Who oft in fear and wonder thither came

To talk with her beneath the garden bowers:
And there amid the brightness of the flowers,
Laughing the child would say,—
"O Lavarcam!
Come, tell me!—Oh come, tell me what I am!
Did I come here just like the summer fly
To sparkle in the sun and then to die?
I've asked the flies full oft, but murmuringly
They said they were too filled of present glee
To give me answer, and they passed away;
And once unto the streamlet did I say
'What am I?'—for in grove or garden walk
I oft feel lonely and perforce must talk
To all things round that creep or walk or fly,
And well I know their speech. And 'What am I?'
I asked the stream; and it was churlish too
And would not speak, but from its weeds upthrew
A great brown frog puffed up with too much pride,
And 'Ugly! Ugly! Ugly!' hoarse he cried;

And then from off the streamlet's grassy brim
He made great mouths at me, and I at him,
Until I grew afeard of him and me,
And ran and ran by bank and rustling tree
Up to the fount to see my gold fish glance,
And with them in the sun like this to dance!" —
Then as a swallow that from o'er the foam
Returns at last to her dear native home,
And filled with joy beneath the branches cool
In airy circles skims her favorite pool,
So round the fountain with light foot and free
The little elfish maid danced gracefully,
Now here, now there, in her wild gambolings
O'er the smooth grass, as if she too had wings!

When nigh ten years had passed, she asked the dame, —
"O Lavarcam, why nam'st thou not my name?
I know it, — Deirdrè! — for one day I heard
Old Caffa mutter it through his great beard.

Art thou afraid of it? Not so am I,
For oft I shout it out so high,—so high,
The wild-birds know it on their topmost tree,
And the wall sends it echoing back to me:
What means it? And why do they keep me
here
Within these high walls shut from year to year?
What means it?"—
Then old Lavarcam replied,
"O dear one, thou shalt be the Great King's bride!"

"A bride!—O Lavarcam, I know that too!
Oft have I seen the little wild-birds woo
Their winsome brides amid the branches green,
And call, and call, 'My Queen! my Queen! my
Queen!'
'Twas only in the early yester morn,
As I sat close beneath yon flowering thorn,
I saw a blue wood-pigeon and his bride
Adown the garden grass walk side by side,

Cooing in gladness as they went along;
Then I stood up and sang their marriage song,
And oh! I sang so loving, loud, and clear,
That the sweet wild-birds joined me far and
near;—
Now tell me, Lavarcam, is this the way
The King and I within his court shall play?
No answer. Then to Caffa I will go,
As he walks brooding in the garden slow,
And ask of him how all these things befel,
For he knows more than mortal tongue can tell!"

Then dancing o'er the sward away went she,
And plucked wise Caffa's robe full wistfully,
And looked into his calm face with a smile
A heart of flinty stone might well beguile:—
"O Caffa, thou hast taught me many a thing,
Why the winds murmur and the tempests ring,
Why 'neath the genial sun the wild flowers bloom,
And why the glittering flies their tints assume;

And thou hast taught my morning orison
To the great God who rules the golden sun,
And how to lift my hands and raise my wail
At Samhain to the Moon so cold and pale,—
Yet thou hast never told me even my name!
But I have heard thee name it, and that shame
And great dishonor and black woe and crime
Shall trouble all the kingdom in my time!—
What am I? And why live I here alone?"

Then Caffa smote his breast, and with a groan
Of sorrow bent on her his pitying eye,
And down the garden strode without reply.

Then ran she till she plucked his gown again,—
"O Caffa, stay! O Caffa, ease my pain!—
Why does the King clothe me in royal dress,
And look on me with such great happiness,—
And gaze and smile, and swear by Sun and Wind
My peer shall ne'er be found 'mongst womankind?

Be sure within this garden fair doth live
Full many a thing that can more comfort give:
My yellow hair is not so full of light
As the gold fish that swim the fountain bright;
My lips were ne'er so fragrant or so red
As the gay roses in yon garden-bed;
And yet the King says they are brighter far,
And that mine eyes are like the morning star!—
What means it?"
With a sigh then Caffa said,
"O guileless little thing! O gold-haired maid!
What boots it aye to thee these things to know?
For thee in joy the seasons come and go.
For thee each day with happiness is fraught,
Then take them as they come, without a thought!"

But she, unsatisfied, plucked at his gown
Again, and, with a face half smile and frown,
Said, "Nay! thou goest not. What brings him here?

What is a King, that his bold looks I fear?
Thou answerest not. Ah! well—ah! well I
know!—
One day in springtime, when the daw and crow,
The finch, the blackbird and the blue-winged jay,
Each unto each their friendly thoughts 'gan say,
Above the trees a whirring sound I heard,
And in the sky I saw the eagle bird
Come hither from the far-off mountains bare,
Cleaving with mighty wings the middle air;
And, as he came, all living things were mute.
The weasel sought the old tree's gnarlèd root,
The hare hid 'neath her fern, the garden-mouse
Tumbled with sudden fright into its house,
And every brooding bird upon her nest
Laid closer to her young her downy breast,
Until he passed away in headlong speed.
'Ha! ha!' I said, 'thou art a king indeed!'"

One stilly day, 'neath autumn's amber beam,
She sat with Lavarcam beside the stream,

And looked upon the leaves that strewed the ground
In fading pomp and glory all around,
And said, —
"O Lavarcam, and shall I be
Like these poor castaways of bush and tree?
I've seen them bloom on many a branch and stem,
And I have bloomed, and why not die like them!
Thou hast not died, for the Gods understood
My hapless case, and they were kind and good,
And left thee as my sole companion here,
Whom I can always love without a fear!"

At this the old dame's look grew soft and kind,
Her heart swelled and with tears her eyes were blind,
And close she drew the maid, and fondly pressed
The blooming bosom to her withered breast.

"Alas! and woe is me! thou winsome maid,
Why speak of death in thy bright bloom?" she said,

"And why perplex thy heart and cloud thy brain,
And rive my bosom with thy questions vain?
Why think these thoughts of woe? Ah! rather
quaff
Thy cup of early joy, and dance and laugh
And gambol while thou may'st, for soon enough
Thy skies may darken and thy paths grow rough;
And yet, perchance, the mighty Gods who sit
On their bright thrones, and see the centuries flit
Like shadows by before their golden gate,
May yet relent and weave a happier fate
For thee, belov'd, when thou goest forth a queen
Into the world by thee as yet unseen!"

One day the King came and with Caffa talked,
As down the garden, side by side, they walked:—
"O Caffa, now what boots thy prophecy?
What harm hath come to Eman and to me
For having of my will in this small thing?
See yonder, merrier than the birds that sing,

She sports and gambols round the garden bright
In her young innocence and fresh delight!—
What harm?"
"O King," said Caffa, "nothing yet.
Her day will come, and thine, of black regret
And unavailing tears and bitter woe.
But see how with her radiant cheeks aglow
She turns and comes to sift us once again
With queries wisdom's craft will fight in vain!"

Up came she glittering 'mid the garden blooms,
Like some gay orient bird of gorgeous plumes,
Airy and graceful, glorious to behold,
Bright smiling in her sheeny robes of gold.
Then to her softly said the King in play,
"What sport hadst thou in this sweet spot to-day?"

"I played but with myself, and that with fear;
For all the birds were sullen, thou being here,

And would not sing for me!" the maid replied.

Then the King laughed, and 'twixt half-wounded pride
And wonder spoke again, "What hast thou not,
O maid, that thou complainest of thy lot?
Of this fair place, — this house and garden green, —
And all its merry creatures, thou art queen.
What wantest thou?"
Then she replied, "O King,
Long time the wild-birds' songs to me would bring
But joy, yet now mixed up in every note
Some tone of sadness to my heart will float.
Long time I laughed; but now, I know not why,
Their warbling songs both make me laugh and cry.
And, as I grow and grow, mine eyes can view
Things different from what my childhood knew.
The other day, a linnet's family
I saw full happy in the birchen tree.

Then sudden came the hawk, and spoiled the nest,
And slew the young, while with blood-dabbled breast
The wounded mother on the sward lay tost,
Fluttering, and wailing for the loved ones lost.
Then into my dimmed eyes the salt tears came,
And something burned within my heart like flame;
And wild I clapped my hands and smote my brow,
And cried, 'O mother! mother! where art thou
To watch and wail me when mine hour is come,
Like these poor birds?'—O King, what hapless
doom
Is on me?"
Then the King: "Nought but the best
Of fortune on thy golden head shall rest,
While I am King and sit upon the throne;
And thou within my heart shalt reign alone,
And thou shalt see the great bright world outside."

Then sudden changed her mood, and, "Oh!" she
cried,

"I saw it once, and I will tell thee how.
One day, as I sat 'neath the beechen bough,
I saw a little squirrel climb the tree,
Sit on a branch, and eye me roguishly.
These were my glad times, and the squirrel gay
Amid the branches green did seem to say,
With wild bright eyes, and bushy tail upcurled,
'Come up! come up! come up, and see the world!'
And up I clomb the green tree after him,
Higher, and higher still, from limb to limb,
Till from the topmost boughs at length I gazed
Over the garden wall, and then half-dazed
With wonder saw I the great world spread out
That Lavarcam tells all the tales about!
And first upon a gentle sloping hill
I saw a sight, and seem to see it still, —
With all its moats and towers, a palace great,
And a strong band of heroes from its gate
Issuing upon the broad white gleaming road
That from the palace leads by this abode.

Now broader streamed their banner's silken fold,
And brighter flashed their harnesses of gold,
As nearer by our gateway they did come,
With loud brass clashing and great roar of drum.
And on their front came riding side by side
Three youthful knights in all their martial pride,
With red cloaks fluttering in the summer breeze
And gay gems flashing on their harnesses,
And on the helm that guarded each proud head,
And on each shield where shone the Branch of Red.
And, as they passed, the eldest of the three
With great black wistful eyes looked up at me;
For he did mark this yellow head of mine
Amid the green tree's branches glint and shine,
And oh! the look,—the fond bright look he
gave!"

Then flushed the King's brow like an angry wave
That rises wallowing from the storm-vexed sea
Under a blood-red sunset threateningly.

Then Caffa started, and with troubled look
Full dolefully his withered head he shook,
And muttered to himself, "The poisoned knife
Hath gleamed at last for Eman's woe and strife,
For the king's heart and Usna's noble sons!"

While heedlessly as the blithe streamlet runs
The maid went on, unweeting of the pain,—
"And then they passed, and then I looked again.
And oh! the sight I saw, the woodlands gay,
The windy moorlands, and the mountains gray,
The world's great shining plains spread out so far,—
Oh! farther than the slender glittering bar
Of cloud that oft in windless nights of June
Lies like a golden lance athwart the moon!"

And thus she questioned them, and told the smart
That 'gan to prey on her young budding heart,
Till sixteen slender years away had flown
Over her golden head, and she had grown

Owner of all the beauty that once graced
Eirè and Banba, Fœla, and the chaste
Credè of Anann's Paps, and gay Ailleen
Of Leinster, and the young Momonian Queen,
Moria, and the Danann Goddesses;
Una of Irian woods and bloomy leas;
Ainè the Fair, the Brightness of the grass;
And Samhain mild, who holds the Moon's pale glass;
Sad Cliona, ruler of the Southern storm;
And regal Fincave of the Sun-bright form;
And Aevin, Guardian of Kincora's gate;
And Amarac the Wise and Fortunate!

THE FLIGHT FROM EMAN.

CALM Autumn died, and in that garden fair
The last flowers withered in the treacherous air.
The little stream with mournful murmurs rolled,
And the trees doffed their robes of bronze and gold,
And fading blue and green, and glowing red;
And all the outside lands lay damp and dead,
Wrapped in a cheerless shroud of foggy haze,
Voiceless for lengths of dreary days on days,
Save now and then through the dull gloom was heard
The wierd-like warning of the drummer-bird,
The bittern, from the flat isles of the mere,
Or curlew's calling, now remote, now near,

Or the wild plover from the upland springs,
Or mighty whirr of multitudinous wings
Of rooks and noisy starlings spreading o'er
The cattle pastures by the river-shore.
And sometimes, too, the ruffian winds would come
To chase the dying leaves from their last home
In the forlorn grove, or with dread sound
The Thunder God would rise from underground
And roar amid the gaps of distant hills,
And the thick rain would pour and swell the
rills
To rivers, and the rivers into seas,
Till all at once would rise a southern breeze,
Born 'mid the bowers of some more genial clime,
And make a mimic summer for a time.

But soon all soft airs died, and from between
The east and north a strong wind blew full keen
For many a day, and from the steely sky
The sun deceptive let his arrows fly

On bank and brake, and without heat to fall
Ev'n 'gainst the garden's gleaming southern wall;
And colder still it blew, till one bright morn
It lulled awhile. Upon the spreading thorn
The field-fares bickered at the ruddy haw,
The last fruit of the year; the thievish daw
Fought on the palace gable with his wife;
And the fierce magpie, born to ceaseless strife,
Swung on the larch and told his household woes,
Or plumed his tail and threatened all his foes
With vicious screams and angry rhapsodies;
And loud the finches chirruped in the trees;
While, high o'er all, in blue, thin columns broke
From the tall chimney-tops the palace smoke.
All things shone crisp and cold, till from the sea,
Between the east and north, rose gradually
A great gray woolly cloud, that grew and grew
Voluminous, till from the ether blue
It blotted out the sun ere evening's hour,
And wrapt the ghostly garden, tree and bower,

In its thick folds obscure. Then from on high,
To earth slow spiralling adown the sky,
The first great feathery snow-flakes made their way,
Till all the garden changed from black to gray,
From gray to white. Then rose the wind again
From the fell North and growled against the pane
And round the house, and each successive blast
As the night fell grew stronger than the last,
Till, as the great whales, gathered in a shoal,
In some far bay anear the shining pole,
Gambol in thunder, while the waters boil
Around them like the Maelstrom's whirling coil,
And high to heaven the sheeted foam-wreaths toss,
So that strong wind amidst the feathery floss
Of falling snow wallowed the livelong night,
Tumultuous, till at length the morning light
Rose calm and clear, and upward sprang the sun,
And with his level beams serenely shone
On the soft snow robe that lay white and pure
O'er glade and splendid hill and dazzling moor.

On this first virgin day of wintry sheen,
When round the glittering garden nought was green,
Save where the snow slipt from the lofty pine,
Or where the gelid leaves half-black would shine
Through the white wreaths upon the laurel shade,
At her bower window musing sat the maid,
With Lavarcam beside her. On her knee
With listless hand she held her broidery
Of golden woof.
"O thou, my bosom's friend,"
At length she said, "when comes the weary end
Of this most weary life? Alas, in vain
To change this dull existence I am fain.
See yonder, by the warm side of the brake,
How the sleek hares their morning revels make,
And toss the snow around them in their play.
Ev'n these poor things,—these have their merry day,
And live and die in freedom. And must I
In ceaseless durance live, in prison die?

Ah! rather, — but behold how from afar
The king-bird comes these creatures' sport to mar! —
Look! look! O Lavarcam!"
They looked, and saw
The eagle of the golden beak and claw
And bronze-bright feathers shadowy overhead,
And silent on the elastic ether spread
A space, or with alternate flutterings
Beating the light air with his winnowing wings;
While, underneath, the quick hares 'gan to flee
Into the brake, save one that tremblingly
Crouched blind with fear. Then, as when 'cross the heaven
On a wild March day the dark wrack is driven,
And a small cloud-rent sails athwart the sun,
Sudden a bright gleam smites the marshland wan,
Arrowy and swift, so like that flash of light
The mighty king-bird from the heavenly height
Shot down upon the shuddering prey below
With a great whirr that raised the powdery snow

In a pale cloud around, and from that cloud
His piercing mort-scream echoed shrill and loud
Upon the listeners' ears; then with his prey
Up through the blue bright heaven he sailed away,
Leaving upon the snow a broad red streak
Of blood behind him.
With a tremulous shriek
Then Deirdrè clapped her hands and cried, "Ah me!
Alas! alas! what marvels do I see
Of woe and death within this fated place!"
And then she wept awhile, till with a face
All smiles and courtliness the old dame spoke:—

"O maid! why weepest thou? The eagle's stroke
Fell on its natural prey, no more. But look
How from the great oak-tree beside the brook
Yon raven lights, and round the blood doth dance,
And stops, and eyes it eagerly askance,

And drinks it!—Ha! thou shudderest at the
 sight
And weepest still. But see these colors bright,
The blood's fresh scarlet in the morning beam,
The raven's plumage with its inky gleam,
Blending together, and how gay they show
Upon the sunlit sheet of pearly snow.
Child of my heart's best love! ah, rather think,
Not of the bloody draught the bird will drink,
But of these glorious colors when they grace
All beautiful some brave young prince's face,—
The raven's black on eyebrows, beard, and hair,
On teeth and skin the snow's white brilliance fair,
The red blood's splendor on bright lips and cheeks,
And thou the lady his fond bosom seeks!"

Then Deirdrè grew full pale, and in her eyes
There came a look half terror, half surprise,
Till from her beating heart the blood returned,
And o'er her face the brightening blushes burned

Up to the roots of her soft yellow hair,
Then low she sighed and said, —
"Why mock my care,
O Lavarcam! with thoughts that thou wilt find
But as weak visions of thy sanguine mind?
I, but the King's poor chattel, — I to think
Of such great happiness!"
"From the sweet brink
Of the King's cup of joy unto his lip,"
Said Lavarcam, "there may be many a slip,
As the old saw doth say. A King's control
In slavish chains can bind no freeborn soul.
'Like unto like' is still a maxim sage;
Youth unto blooming youth, and age to age.
As well might this old withered heart of mine
For some gay noble of the palace pine,
As the King seek thy love. But I have vowed
No heart-break sad thy life's young morn shall cloud.
And I have chosen for thee a noble knight,
Young, beautiful, and brave; in all things bright

As those fair-shining colors that we see.
And thou must love him well, for he loves thee!"

"I cannot love but one," replied the maid,
"And he — I know him not!" and sore afraid,
And blushing still, she led the aged crone
Into another room more still and lone,
And sat her down, and there with guileless art
Poured forth the confidence of her young
heart;
And told her of the well-remembered day
She heard the drums and saw the pageant gay
March down the palace road, and of the knight
Of the black locks and loving glances bright,
And regal bearing, and lithe, graceful limb;
And how within her heart she thought of him
Through all that long time; while with twinkling
eyes
The wily beldame feigned a new surprise
At every word, and when the maid was done, —

"Oh! wonderful!" she cried: "the very one—
The very self-same knight I've chosen for thee!
Naisi, the flower of Emān's chivalry,
Great Usna's son and cousin of the King;
And him and you together I will bring,
If fortune smiles, in garden, grove, or vale,
Where you may utter forth your mutual tale
And open your young hearts; and may the Gods
Look smiling on you from their blest abodes,
And watch and ward you from all sore distress,
And give you long, sweet days of happiness!"

Straightway to Naisi the young Red Branch Knight
Went Lavarcam, and filled him with delight,
As well she told, with voluble display
Of her well-practised tongue, how night and day
Young Deirdrè thought of him, and him alone!
And to and fro she went as time rolled on
Full secretly, till long ere spring's return
Their hearts with love's hot fires began to burn.

And now within the gilded palace room
Was not one look or word or sigh of gloom
From Deirdrè, as the happy, heavenly time
Of love's first dawning brightened towards its prime,
The hour that by the old dame's subtle art
Would bring them face to face and heart to heart.

And all things now she looked upon before
With thoughts full sad, a different aspect wore,
Transformed and brightened by love's genial
ray;
And when the King came on a certain day,
So boundless was her joy, she smiled on him
With radiant face, and eyes no longer dim.
Whereat the glad King rubbed his jewelled hands,
And swore by all the gods of seas and lands
To marry her that moment he was fain.
And, as he went, be sure that ne'er again
So light his golden-sandalled feet would pass
As on that morning through the gate of brass.

Now Winter died the windy hills among,
And Spring came singing her delightful song,
And scattering flowers around her as she came,
And flooding all the skies with azure flame.
One balmy day when brightly shone the sun,
And when the King was to his hunting gone
With Conal Carna, where Dunseverick stood,
Perched on its gray rock o'er the ocean flood;
And while they listened to the harp's sweet sound,
And while the gem-bright cups of mead went round,
While the King laughed, while oft his secret mind
Went back to his fair flower of womankind,—
On this calm day, beneath the wildwood tree
Stood Naisi in a glade where murmuringly
The stream sped out with silver-gleaming fall
From underneath fair Deirdrè's garden-wall.
Around him shone the sights of early May,
The golden broom, the hawthorn's blossomed spray,
The daffodils high nodding o'er the grass
Beside the pool that spread like azure glass,

The brakes of green where birds began to sing
And each to each make love with twittering
wing,
The blue-bell drooping o'er its slender stem,
The daisy shining like a silver gem
Amidst the fragrant grass. And bright as they
Looked Naisi in his princely garments gay:
On his proud head a birrèd green he bare,
Rimmed round with pearls, whence flowed his raven
hair,
A lustrous flood of love-locks smooth and long
Over his brawny shoulders broad and strong.
Unto his tall knee fell his loric's fold
Of crimson woof and fringe of woven gold;
And o'er his swelling breast a belt was flung,
And from its clasp a mighty falchion hung
In its long sheath that, like a serpent's scale,
Glittered with emerald and the silver pale.
At his strong hip an ancient dirk he wore,
That on its scabbard the brave semblance bore

Of his great race,—an Osprey fierce and proud,
Resistless swooping from a stormy cloud.
And at each motion that the hero made
The sun smiled on him, lightening all the glade
With golden flashes and blue glimmerings
From cloak and arms and baldric's studs and rings.

Graceful he leant upon his javelin shaft,
And often to himself full low he laughed
With joy, as love's deep fountain bubbled up
From his great heart, like sweet wine o'er its cup
Poured by a generous hand. Oft-times he eyed
With eager look the green glade's bosky side;
For on that day old Lavarcam had said
Young Deirdrè should walk down the woodland glade,
Freed for the moment by her subtle tongue
From the sharp nurse's watching. And not long
Looked Naisi, till amid these bowers of spring
He saw his loved one's garments glittering

In the soft sunny light that seemed to throw
Around her face divine a triple glow
Of glory to his eyes, as she drew near.
And not with throbbing heart of doubtful fear,
Nor yet with trembling limbs and sidelong eye,
She stepped into the glade, but proud and high,
And bold in her white innocence she came
Before him, wondering at his mighty frame,
And the fair fashion of his martial dress,
And gleaming arms, and his great comeliness.
A space she beamed on him her glorious eyes
In happiness of heart and mute surprise,
Then cried, —
"Ah! well I know that thou art he
I saw long syne from out the beechen tree,
Mine own belov'd that I have kept enshrined
Within my constant heart and lonely mind!"

Said Naisi: "O thou maid, stretch forth thine hand
That I may feel thy presence warm and bland,

That I may think thee not a vision sweet,
A phantom that mad knights in wildwoods meet!"

Then hand met hand; and, as they touched, great fears
Disturbed her heart, and rose the shining tears
Into her violet eyes, as well she thought
How near destruction's sharp brink they were brought
By keeping of their tryst.

"Alas! alas!"
She cried, "must Caffa's dread words come to pass,
And must we two, in our fair youthful bloom,
For loving of each other meet our doom?
Speak to me, love! Am I not all to thee?"

Then Naisi's dark eyes lightened lovingly
Upon her, as he answered, —

"Thou art mine
For evermore, belov'd! And I am thine

For evermore; and whether we may shun
Our doom or not, our hearts, O love, are one
In life or death!"

Then from her forehead fair
She brushed a silken ripple of bright hair
That from the flood of her rich tresses stole,
And looked with wordless love into his soul,
And said,—

"Now, Naisi, I can bear the worst,—
Death in its many shapes, the desert's thirst,
The dungeon's hunger, or the burning stake,
Unfearing and unflinching for thy sake!"

Then Naisi straightened high his martial form,
And with love's ardor grew his heart full warm
And sanguine that all things were fair and
good.
And there, as in that sunny glade they stood,
All-beautiful they seemed as glorious Nied,
The War-God, and his ever-blooming bride,

Bava, within the heaven beyond the hills!
And now forgetting all the pains and ills
That threatened them, they talked of love
alone,
Heart unto heart, till nigh their hour had flown,
And from their fond dream they awoke. Again
She thought of all the peril and the pain
And woe and desolation that should fall
Upon herself, on Naisi, and on all,
Because she could not love the King, and how,
Some dreadful dȧy of days, with truthful brow
To tell the King that she did love him not,
That with young Naisi she had cast her lot,
For ever and for ever, hap what might!
And Naisi saw the quenching of the light
Within her eyes at the recurring thought,
And said,—
"From this sweet hour our fate is wrought,
And we are linked in one, and have achieved
The end we wished for, that our souls believed

Would never come, — O love, we two have met!
Then cast all fear aside and black regret
Unto these wandering winds that whisper by.
For what care you, O maid, and what care I,
For danger in our all-absorbing love?"

Then with her fears young Deirdrè's bosom strove
A moment, and away the dark thoughts fled;
And he looked in her trusting eyes, and said, —

"O love, beyond King Connor's boundaries
There stretch broad kingdoms, and great billowy
seas
Murmur in many winds, and we can fly,
And refuge take beneath some foreign sky,
If the worst comes; and Ainli, Ardan, brave,
My brothers, with us too will cross the wave
In our strong-masted galleys, whose white sails
Spread their broad sheets to Moyle's tempestuous
gales,

Far, far away unto some gallant shore
Where Danger lurks and Valor stalks before,
Where we will cross wild mountains, moors, and
fords,
And conquer some great kingdom with our swords!
And there, O Deirdrè! we shall wear the crown
And drink our fill of love and earth's renown,
And tread our own glad halls by wrath unbanned,
Far from the vengeance of King Connor's hand!"

They parted, and she sought her palace home;
While Naisi lingered, with glad heart to roam
The glades awhile, and thought no eyes could
see
Their trysting 'neath the bloomy wildwood tree.

Yet on that trysting glared a savage look
From out the tangled brake beside the brook,
Where like a wounded wolf whose rage is strong
Close lurked in silence all the mid-day long

Maini, a King's son of far Norroway,
Who dwelt in Eman 'neath King Connor's sway,
Whose sire and two strong brothers in the fight
Had fallen 'neath Naisi's sword of matchless might,
Beyond the surge on Bora's field of gore.
And now he watched brave Naisi evermore
Full treacherously, as is the caitiff's wont
Who fears to meet a brave man at the front,
But comes behind, and stabs ere he can see.
Hid in his lies, he watched full warily,
Nursing his wrath: as in the woody glen
The wild-cat walks around its darksome den
Within some hollow trunk with velvet feet,
And the great bear, to taste the morning sweet,
Comes forth beside the lonely-sounding stream;—
The wild-cat's voice is mute, his green eyes gleam
With fury, while the royal bear goes by,
Unconscious of the small foe lurking nigh!—
So watched he Naisi, and so Naisi went
His ways, unmindful of his discontent

And deadly hate, and now this noontide fair
He looked from out the copse with vengeful glare
Upon the lovers; and, when all was done,
Through the gay wildwood 'gan to skulk and run
From copse to leafy copse, until unseen
He reached the hero-peopled palace green.
There with vague hints and nods and looks of bale
Around bright Eman's green he spread the tale
Full secret, as when, 'mid the forest, gleams
A quiet crystal pool, unfed by streams;
Silent it lies with all its images
Of painted blossoms and sky-piercing trees
And reeds and rocks, till from its oozy bed
The otter sudden rears his murderous head,
Looks round a moment on the glassy plain,
Then turns, and dives and disappears again;
Around the spot disturbing wavelets flow
And to the banks in widening circles go.
Like the fell otter Maini crept amid
The palace folk, and in his wiles was hid;

Like the wave circles widening as they sprung,
Spread the black venom of his bitter tongue!

Now, when the King returned, his heart was glad,
For in the North a merry time he had
With Conal Carna and his joyous cheer,
Sweet harp and feast and hunting of the deer.
And now his thoughts came back unto the maid,
And in gay garments royally arrayed
He sought her bower and found no brightening eyes,
But looks of dread, and tears, and sad replies,
And knew not what to think, and called apart
The Seer, and told him of his rankling smart;
Whereat the old man shook his hoary head
And spoke,—
"O mighty King, when love is dead,
No art of man can make it bloom again!"

And when the King, 'mong all his glittering train,
Walked moody 'cross the palace green, he saw
Two varlets quarrelling their weapons draw,

One for Clan Usna, one for Eman's King;
And when he sought the cause of this strange thing
The glooming brows around a tale could tell
Whose meaning in his heart he guessed too well.

Then waxed he full of wrath and threatening
gloom,
And with the nobles sought the banquet room
To drown the rage and rancor of his soul
With the harp's music and the brightening bowl.
But vain his wish; for, as the wine rose high
And flushed his cheeks, full oft a baleful eye
He cast on Usna's sons adown the board,
That told more eloquent than brandished sword
Of savage vengeance and immortal hate.
And from that day contention and debate,
And secret whispers and loud bickerings,
And hostile glances, and the word that stings
The bosom and estranges friend from friend,
Arose in Eman, till the bloody end

Seemed nigh of Maini's plot to slay his foe.
And as the wild winds o'er the ocean blow
And fan the rolling surges, so this thing
Uplashed the rising passions of the King
Into a threatening storm of fury strong;
And gage met gage, and wrong succeeded wrong,
Till in the middle of a windy night
From the King's palace Usna took its flight,
The high-souled, noble, loud-war-thundering clan,
Banner and tent, horse, chariot, maid, and man!
And with them Deirdrè went. Howe'er 'twas done,
Within the palace none could tell save one,
Old Lavarcam, and she with eyes upturned
Clapped loud her withered hands, and wildly mourned,
With seeming grief and artful-feigned distress,
The lovers' wicked flight, yet none the less
From hall and banquet-room she kept away,
And shunned the moody King for many a day!

THE WELCOME TO THE MANSION OF KETH.

UPON the rich verge of the northmost plain
That owned great Mab and Olild's prosperous reign,
And frowning 'gainst a mountain gap whose side
A great wood robed in all its shaggy pride,
A fortress stood, the strong-spear-bristling shield
Of many a hamlet, many a fruitful field,
That lay around, from Ulad's borderers free,
And fierce Fomorian rovers of the sea.
One autumn eve upon the watch-tower height
Stood the great stronghold's captain, Keth the knight,
And looked with pride upon the realm that lay
Rich, populous, and fertile 'neath his sway:

The merry village with its sheltering trees,
The peaceful cattle browsing o'er the leas,
The hardy shepherd whistling on the plain
With his white flock, by fields of ripened grain
That lay in golden billows 'neath the hook
Of the brown reaper.

By the bubbling brook
That nigh the strong fort sang its melody,
With scarlet berries laughed the rowan tree,
The nuts in clusters from the hazels hung,
And high and wide the stately oak-tree flung
Its fretted branches rich with acorns brown;
While from a leafless spray anigh its crown,
A brown thrush sang his song with dulcet throat
Betimes awakening the glad redbreast's note
Responsive from its thorny brake whereon
The blackberries like living garnets shone.
Nigh on the moor the milkmaids clinked their cans
And sang their songs, where gleamed the diamond
vans

Of myriad gnats in the sun's slanting beam;
And by the borders of the widening stream
The bog-flax drooped its head of silvery snow,
And the last iris shone with golden glow,
And yellow sun-flowers closed their drowsy
lids,
While far away the mountains' pyramids,
Clad in their heathery robes of purple bright,
Towered heavenward in the rosy sunset light.

As the knight looked, his heart began to fill
With gladness at the scene so fair and still;
For sweet is peace to him who knoweth war.
And long he gazed and thought, till from afar,
Beyond the mountain gap there rose a sound
Like angry torrents rumbling underground
Through a deep caverned hill; then to his ear
Came a great battle shout distinct and clear
Rolling along the plain, and, as it rolled,
The shepherd urged his white flock to the fold,

The milkmaids trembling fled, the herding men
With loud cries drove their cattle to the pen,
And to their homes the reapers hurried fast.
Then Keth upon his war-horn blew a blast,
Whose rolling echoes scarce had died away,
When round the high walls flashed his stern array
Of shielded, saffron-kilted soldiery.
Upon his horn another blast blew he,
Loud-echoing, ringing shrill, and at the note
Full many a charger's hoof the pavement smote
With sounding clang, as on the level space
Of the broad green the horsemen took their place,
And charioteers, a bright brass-glittering line
Whereon the evening cast its dazzling shine,
Blazing on round-rimmed shield and plumèd head,
And tipping all the spear-points crimson red.
Proudly he looked upon the gallant show
Of mail-clad knights upon the sward below,
And bearded soldiers ranged around the wall;
Then on his horn he blew a last long call,

And at the sound came striding up the stair,
Brass-panoplied, his henchman, Brann the Fair,
Crying, "Brann the Henchman here to do thy hest!"
And as a host who meets a well-loved guest
With fair face smiling, Keth began to say,—

"O Brann, dost hear the thunder of the fray
Beyond the pass?—Was ever earthly nook
Free a life's span from War's keen pruning-hook?
Yes! by my hand of valor! Ours shall be
From plundering foes and war's red carnage free,
While I can wield the sword that dealeth death!—
But hark! I hear the war-horn's stormy breath
Making the still eve shudder with its blare,
Telling that all is ready!"
Down the stair,
With tall Brann clattering in his harness bright,
Unto his lordly chamber went the knight
To arm himself. Thence in his garb of war
Glittering he strode unto his armèd car,—

His great war-chariot with its coal-black steeds
Sleek from sweet corn and grass of flowery meads
Danonian ; then he mounted, while the rein
Brann took in his strong hand, and then amain
The great knight's voice like a loud trumpet pealed
Along the bristling ranks, and fast they wheeled,
Chariots and horsemen, with loud thundering clang
That round the high-piled earthen ballium rang,
And through the rattling gateway of the Dun
Stone-splintering, dust-revolving, out they spun!

There rose a mound anear the hollow pass,
Tufted with trees and green with emerald grass,
Whereby the path ran winding, — from whose
crest
The shaggy gorge lay open to the east,
And to its breezy summit sped the knight
With his fierce followers to o'erlook the fight.
High swelled the hero's mighty heart to see
Beneath him, in the sun, gleam radiantly

A strong band marching towards him, with their
spears
Circling a throng of restless charioteers
And steeds, and rumbling chariots that bare
The matrons, children, and the maidens fair
Of a great tribe, and, like the costly gem
That sparkles on a king's gay diadem,
Amidst them all a gilded chariot drawn
By two white steeds. Then far o'er brake and lawn,
Where oped the deep gorge on the outward plain,
He saw the stubborn fight where still the rain
Of arrows clattered thick, and where the dead
Lay thick beneath o'er many a green glade spread,
For there, victorious, yet another band
Of warriors lifted high the gory hand,
Pursuing of their foes that, scattered wide,
'Neath sword and shaft and brazen javelin died!

Now when the nearer band slow marching wound
Out from the devious valley towards the mound,

And still drew nearer, the Connacian knight
Saw that the chariot with the steeds of white
Bore two young damsels garmented in green
And saffron robes, sitting with mournful mien
Beside a queenly lady fresh and young,
Lovelier than e'er by mortal bard was sung.
Drooping she sat, with elbow on her knee
And sad face on her hand dejectedly;
And oft she sighed, and oft the silent tears
Welled from her large blue eyes, for full of fears
And lorn she looked, as if her anxious mind
Dwelt on some well-belovèd one behind
In the fierce battle-wrack.

Before the band
Two spear-lengths, with a look of high command
And battle's flame still burning in his eye,
A young knight strode, whose head two hand-
breadths high
O'ertopped his followers' heads, with locks of brown
Over his golden gorget curling down,

And firm-set mouth, and sun-tanned swarthy skin,
And beard of ruddy brown on lip and chin.
Haughty he strode and looked. As he came on,
Fierce in his mighty panoply he shone
Of high-ridged brazen helm and linkèd mail,
That oft had cast aside the rattling hail
Of arrows from his broad breast and great heart;
Of orbèd shield that, wrought with curious art,
In gold work on its field for blazon wore
The semblance of a mighty forest boar
Rushing with bristling back from out his den,
Deep in the wood, on struggling dogs and men;
Of ponderous sword hung low upon his thigh,
Whose huge hilt sparkled like a starlit sky
With many a gem; of spear whose dreadful blade,
All battle-notched, of swarthy bronze was made,
Whose tapering shaft in beauty once bloomed bright
A fair young ash by old Ardsalla's height,—
Oft 'mid its green leaves in the happy spring
Did the winds whisper and the wild-birds sing,

Oft 'neath its shadow on the daisied grass
The lovers fond their blissful hours would pass, —
Now — hapless change! — instead of leaves and
buds
Gleamed rings and brazen clasps and silver studs,
And that terrific blade wherefrom the blood,
As down the echoing path the hero strode,
Still dript upon the shaft with ruddy hue.
And when anigh the mound the hero drew,
Halting his band, he strode a step more nigh,
And bent on Keth the knight his fearless eye,
And said, —
"O princely man of bright array,
Stand you as friend for friend to guard the way
With your strong-shielded men? If you do not,
Then speak, that, while our battle blood is hot,
We may acquit us, as our need demands,
Against your might, like good men of our hands!"

Then Keth made answer stoutly: "We oppose
Into this land the coming of all foes

To royal Mab and Olild. Peace is here
Throughout this fertile plain by sword and spear
Well guarded, and all rovers must beware
That death may bar their entrance."
High in air
The stranger raised his mighty brass-bound spear,
And turned him round, and with loud voice and clear
Spoke to his followers their tall files to close:
Then hoarse on either side a tumult rose
Of hostile preparation, like the roar
Of winds in piney woods, or on the shore
The sound of waves remurmuring in the night!
And stern beside the mound had raged the fight
'Tween these strong bands of heroes, had not she,
That lady fair, descended tremblingly
From the bright car and through the bristling files
Glided with weary step and tearful smiles
Unto her champion's side, and spoke, —
"O thou,

Brave brother of my heart, this angry brow
Why wear'st thou? See yon kingly man. His
face
Of wrath or hostile purpose hath no trace.
Poise back thy spear, and speak to him and tell
Thy name and kin, and whatsoe'er befell
To us upon our peril-haunted way
Unto his land. Perchance this closing day
Through him may find us rest a little while!"

Upon the champion's face there beamed a smile
Of kindness as he answered, "For thy sake,
O sister fair, my strong resolve I break
To fight my way into yon fertile plain."

Then to Keth turning, thus he spoke again:
"O man of noble port and regal eye!
My name is Ardan, of the lineage high
Of Usna; and this lady young and bright
Is Deirdrè, wife of Naisi, the good knight,

My brother. If you look beyond the pass,
And hear the shouts and see the gleam of brass,
There he and Ainli with our valiant clan
Fight Eman's men, and conquer, man to man!—
Twelve times the silver moon full-orbed hath shone
From the blue heavens our perilous path upon,
And twelve times waned, since that dread fateful
hour
We reft from Eman's King this loveliest flower
Of all bright beauty and sweet womanhood.
And many a weary day by field and flood
And broad stream-runnelled plain, since that wild
night,
We saw; for when we clomb the northmost height
Above a bay where Moyle with foamy lips
Kisses the rock-strewn beach, we saw our ships
Far blazing; for the King's host, first to gain
The way before us, reached that troublous main
And fired them swift. Then west by north we
turned,
For the bold hopes that in our bosoms burned

To reach fair Alba's shore were dead and gone;
And from hot daylight's glare to starlight wan
No rest, no safety, no strong shield, we knew,
Save in the valiant swords we manful drew
From moon to moon, by blood-stained ford and glen
And treacherous pass, against King Connor's men.
And many a faithful heart behind we left
By ford and hollow pass, of life bereft;
But we had friends, and many a well-armed man
Joined us by secret ways and swelled our clan,
So that the King's men, fighting day by day,
Had all they wished of sword and javelin play,
And turned them from our dangerous path of gore
One wild March morn, anigh the murmuring shore
Where Torry's wave the mainland leaps upon.
There in a bay the fluttering ensigns shone
Of the Fomorian King, from his tall fleet
Of black-hulled galleys that from feet to feet
Of two high headlands shadowed all the wave.
And thereunto a man we sent, to crave

Of the Fomorian passage o'er the sea
To Alba's friendly shore; but scarce had he,
Our herald, trod the King's broad ship and said
His message, when we saw his hoary head
Lopped from his shoulders, and his bleeding
 trunk
Tossed from the poop and in the green sea sunk,
For answer! Then each warrior drew his blade,
And on its hilt our vow of vengeance made;
And like a troop of wolves whose greedy eyes,
Sparkling with famine's fire, behold their prize,
Long sought for, safe within the high-walled pen,
Guarded by watchful dogs and well-armed men,—
Furious they rush for other pens and folds!—
By wild untrodden ways, by hills and wolds,
Bravely we strove our fortunes to renew;
Fighting for bread the weary summer through,
Till on this eve, anigh thy peaceful plain
The King's host fell upon us once again.
Thou see'st the rest. We want but sleep and food!"

Then Deirdrè spoke: "I augur nought but good,
O mighty prince, from thee, for in thine eyes
I see the thoughts that from thy great heart rise;
And thou wilt succor us, for we have dreed
Great misery, and sore hath been our need;
And we are weary, struggling mile by mile;
And I would fain get rest a little while!"

Then Keth: "Within our mighty high-walled dun
Are many mansions, and the brightest one
Of all shall be thy home, O lady fair,
To rest awhile and feel contentment there.
And thou, good knight and bold, thy brothers brave
And valiant clan no more a home shall crave,
While on my hearth the crackling fagots glow,
While I have lands and honors to bestow,
And in gay Cruchaun Mab and Olild reign."

Therewith he bade an old knight of his train
Adown the dusty way to lead them on,
And give them rest and welcome in the Dun.

Now sank the sun upon his ocean bed
In a great blaze of gold and purple red,
And rose the moon and lit with paly ray
Between two forkèd hills the landscape gray,
And all the shrill sounds of the long daylight
Seemed muffled 'neath the drowsy plumes of night.
Still on the mound stood Keth, and through the gloom
With sharp eyes tried to pierce the valley's womb;
For he had sent a warrior of the band
To bid the Usnanians welcome to his land,
And there abode their coming. Like the bells
Of cattle sounding from the twilight fells,
Unto his ear the clink of harness came;
Then sudden burst into the moon's pale flame
From round a clump of trees the mighty clan,
Their silken banner fluttering in the van
With the great Osprey worked in gold thereon;—
Far spread or serried thick they glimmering shone,

Where'er the moon lit up the open glades,
Gleaming on harness, shields and swords, and
blades
Of brazen javelins, changing momently
Like the pale star-beams on a troubled sea.

Straight as two spear-shafts on that front of pride,
Strode the two noble brothers side by side:
Dark Naisi in his heavy panoply
Of brass and gold; young Ainli to his knee
Robed in a saffron tunic, battle-rent,
That showed beneath the mail shirt, blood besprent
From a fresh wound o'er his strong shoulder-blade
By some deft weapon in the battle made.
Yet stout and cheerily he strode along,
Blithe as a bridegroom at the marriage song;
His tawny hair beneath his helmet's rim
Like pale gold shining in the moonlight dim,
His spear upraised and shield advanced, whereon
The semblance of the fighting Hill-Cat shone:

Onward they came, the while with measured tread
Their strong host seemed to shake the valley's bed;
As when in hot July, when grass is green,
In a great dell Ben-Beola's Paps between,
A mighty herd of mountain kine comes there,
Led by their bulls, and graze the pastures bare,
Till from high slope to slope no blade they find,
And scents of fresher meads come on the wind,
And sleep or waking no contentment brings,
And noon smites hot and sharp the gadfly stings;
Away they rush where'er their monarchs lead
By savage tracks unto the untrodden mead,
And from some hollow gap amid the hills
Burst bellowing on that meadowy place of rills;
So from the gorge, and with a thundering sound,
The Usnanian host drew near the grassy mound,
And raised a shout that rent the moonlit sky,
To answer Keth's kind voice as they went by!

Within Keth's merry mansions they abode
While August's suns upon the green hills glowed.

And all their cares, their hardships and distress,
Seemed now forgotten in their happiness.
And there upon a glad September morn
Within the Dun young Deirdrè's babe was
born,
A lovely man child, and they called him Gaeir.
And from the youthful mother, blooming fair
As a young rose-tree that in garden bowers
Puts forth in early June its tender flowers,
All grief departed, and the sweet content,
The bliss maternal by the good Gods sent,
O'erfilled her heart, as her admiring eyes
Beheld her hope, her glory, and her prize,
Her pearl of all the earth, her little boy,
Laugh on her lap in his awakening joy!

One morn as Naisi by the stronghold's gate
Walked up and down, deep thinking of his state,
He heard of horsehoofs the approaching din,
And saw the royal herald dashing in,

With his fierce escort spurring close behind,
Their long cloaks fluttering in the morning wind.
Straight to Keth's open door the herald sped,
Sprang from his steed, and then with stately tread
Went to the chamber, where he told the knight
News from the Queen, of war, — how on each height
Of Ulad, northward to Moyle's roaring sea,
The far-seen beacons blazed incessantly
For gathering of the tribes, that Eman's King
'Gainst Mab and Olild a great host might bring
For harboring of the proud Usnanian clan.
And soon around the Dun the rumor ran;
And Naisi heard it soon, and went straightway
Unto his host, with grateful heart to say, —

"O Prince, for all the joy and happiness
Thou gav'st us in our need and sore distress
We thank thee as brave men should thank the
brave!
But how can we, Ultonians, draw the glaive

Of anger 'gainst our kinsmen? How can we
Give both fair kingdoms to war's misery?
No! Send the Queen's good herald back again,
And tell her Usna's sons are fearless men,
In whose high hearts the flower of Honor glows
Untarnished through all perils, joys, and woes.
No! There are other lands where valor brings
Increase of honor and rewards of Kings;
And we will seek them, that our noble name
May scape the infamy and during shame
Of kindling in our quarrel War's red fires
Between you and the kingdom of our sires!"

THE CAPTURE OF THE FOMORIAN GALLEYS.

NEXT morn, with friendly partings many a one,
They left the stronghold, and the rising sun
Looked with a kindly eye on their array,
As far they wound upon their westward way.
And with no craven bosoms did they go,
Seeking deliverance, weeping, from their woe,
But with high hearts of youthful hope and pride
That knew not fear, and danger's frown defied,
Onward they marched in their best bravery,
Till on the fifth fair eve the far-off sea
Appeared between two hills to heaven outrolled,
Resplendent 'neath the sunset's burning gold.

Beneath an oak-wood's boughs they camped that
night,
And at the first gleam of the morning light
Bestirred themselves, and lit their fires, and made,
With lively hum beneath the leafy shade,
Their meal of wild-boar chines, — a goodly cheer, —
And quern-ground wheat, and flesh of forest deer
And wine and sparkling water. Then they rose,
And struck their tents, and, thick as corn that grows
Wind-waven on the long ridge after rain,
Glittered their spear-points, as they marched again
Into the great gap 'mid the hills wherethro'
The first bright ocean glimpse had met their view,

At noon they cleared the pass, and saw the main
Smooth gleaming to the far-off skies again,
Beyond a level tract wherein a bay
Curved towards them, all its sunny waves at play
With the sweet winds, as if in mockery
Of man's fell wrath and madness raging nigh ; —

Nigh on the shore, where from a burning town
The smoke clouds rolled away o'er dale and down,
Where red before the Usnanians' wondering gaze
In forkèd tongues uprose the ravenous blaze; —
Whence on the soft breeze came the sounds of woe,
Now rising high and shrill, now falling low,
Heart-rending as the ululations drear
Of a great tribe around its chieftain's bier!

Then shook the ground beneath the forward tread
Of Usna's host, as towards the town they sped
With high hope-burning hearts, — the mighty Three
Striding before their front ranks manfully,
Their shields advanced, until their armèd feet
Plashed through the fresh blood on the ruined street,
Where scattered far the slaughtered people lay,
Maid, mother, father, child and grandsire gray; —
Where all around beneath the smoke clouds dim
The ruined walls loomed up all black and grim, —

Wherein through rose-bright lattices the sun
Looked with glad beams the household folk upon,
Smiling upon their matin revelling,
Unweeting what the dreadful noon would bring!
And now as up the street the host had come
With vengeful pity and strange wonder dumb,
Young Deirdrè from her car that sight of bale
Marked with tear-streaming eyes and cheeks all pale,
And, with protecting arms full closely pressed,
Clasped her dear little son to her fond breast,
Hiding him 'neath her mantle's crimson fold:
While like a fierce bear of the savage wold,
That turns him in the evening's solitude
Unto his den, and finds his woolly brood
And faithful mate dead 'neath the hunter's lance
And weltering yet in gore; with dreadful glance
He stalks around and snuffs the tainted air,
Now growling stern, now darting here and there
His red eye searching for his mortal foe,—
So Naisi in his wrath strode to and fro,

Now gazing on the dead, now through the wrack
Burning to find the fell destroyer's track;
Till as his dark eyes wandered fiercely round,
Beneath a ruined porch a man he found
Old, wounded, with his back propped 'gainst the wall,
And thus the aged carle:—
"O champion tall,
I hail thee, for with dying eyes I see
Our strong avenger thou shalt surely be!
Long were the people of my name and race
Happy in this now hapless, woful place;
For we were traders inland folk between
And the blithe Rovers of the ocean green,
Protected, happy, till last eventide
Some men of Talc came in their cruel pride
Into our town, from where their pirate sails
Are yonder furled, safe from September gales,
Beyond the hill-ridge in a sheltered bay.
Into the town they came, and with wild fray

And riot filled the street, and stabbed the son
Of Elim our good chieftain, whereupon
We rose and slew them. Then the wrath was hot
Of him whose varlets fierce we sparèd not,
Fomorian Talc, the cruel pirate King,
Whose spears have ceased not yet their glittering
In yonder pass. He came. Thou see'st the rest!"

Down drooped the old man's head upon his breast,
And to the Gods his fierce soul cleft the sky!
And Naisi looked, and with dark threatening eye
Beheld afar, two rocky hills between,
Of spears and harnessed backs the moving sheen
Waveward receding, and right joyfully
Struck his great shield and cried, "'Tis he! 'tis he!
Fomorian Talc, the pirate King, who gave
Our herald's headless trunk unto the wave,
That slew this people! — Kindred, follow me!"

He turned, and with a roar full vengefully
The warriors followed his long strides, all fain

For battle, marching 'cross the shoreside plain
And 'tween the hills, until they gained a height
Green-swarded, flat-topped, and with coast flowers
bright,
And sloping to the sea strand. Opposite,
Far as a bow-shaft in its flight could hit,
Arose an island, sea-disparted, steep,
With two long arms outstretched upon the deep,
Enclosing a bright bay whose shining mouth
Oped to the gentle breezes of the south.
Between the flat-topped hillock and the bound
Of the rough isle there lay a shallow sound
Whose waters at the neap-tide rose less high
Than the swarth mail-rings on a warrior's thigh;
And as the Usnanians looked across its tide,
Before them on the wild isle's hither side,
Dread sentinel o'er land and restless sea,
Frowned the Fomorian stronghold gloomily;
While in the sheltered elbow of the bay
Their black-hulled galleys at the anchor lay,

Numerous; as when to some wild island shore
Of Thulè from the north the gannets pour
At breeding time, and strike the arch that spans
The earth and ocean with their whirring vans,
Till settling slowly down upon the deep
They fold their wings, and, rocked in dreamless sleep,
Lie in close pack upon the swelling wave,
So lay the ships. Of hempen coil and stave,
Torn from the ribs of many a stranded bark,
A palisade along the neap-tide mark
Ran by the sound and up the island shore,
Circling the hold. Through this tall fence a door,
Grim with strong bar and boss and seamed with
spray,
For the Fomorian rear-guard open lay.

Upon the height the Usnanians now upraised
The Osprey. Brightly in the sun he blazed
On his gay silken field; then tent by tent,
They pitched their ready camp, and eager went

To the height's verge and looked across its tide
To view their foes. Now either host descried
The other, and from their strong hearts gave forth
A hostile shout ; as when, from out the north,
The Wind-God sends his blasts against an isle
Shaggy with oak and birch for many a mile ;
Fiercely they rise, and on their foamy path
Fan the wild billows into rage and wrath,
And scourge the isle till all its tossing trees
Find tongues of thunder roaring winds and seas
Defiance, while the winds and seas reply
Booming along the shore : so rose the cry
'Tween bitter host and host ; — from isle and height
Flashed all their brandished spears and harness
bright
With dreadful flame ; and hill and hollow shore
Gave back the warlike din !

Now rose once more
The voice of Naisi : "O ye faithful hearts !
The thought that thrills the soul, the tear that starts

Into a true man's eye, come back to me
When I think on your deathless constancy.
Great were our needs and trouble, greater yet
The glorious task to-morrow's end will set
For our brave hands of valor to achieve.
Ah! whatsoever meshes Fate may weave
Around a man whose will is stern and strong,
Her tangles bind around him, but not long:
The Fate-compeller, his hard hand of toil
Nerved by his valiant heart, will burst the coil.
The small white kernel in the woodland nut,
Within its fibrey shell of hardness shut,
When Spring returns, the life within, awake
With Nature's strength, its prison walls will break
To light and bloom! So we. Ah, what a ring
Fate tightened round us since the wrathful King
Pursued us with his vengeance; yet our hands
In each sore trial broke its circling bands
With inborn valor, till on this fair place
We stand with our deliverance face to face.

Fear not the end, for all that earth contains
Is in the brave man's grasp who fear disdains;
And ere a second sun shall gild the flowers,
Yon fleet of pirate galleys shall be ours,
To sail the sea to Alba's pleasant shore
Where the King's wrath can trouble us no more!"

And all that day they rested. Night came on,
And o'er the hostile camps the pale moon shone
Stilly and bright, and 'cross the silent sea
From Usna's hill oft rose wild minstrelsy,
While answering from the isle came savage songs
With clash of cymbals and barbaric gongs,
And frequent jest and gibe, and laugh of scorn
And the low grumbling of the guttural horn;
Till, nigh the third watch, over isle and hill
Deep slumber settled down, and all was still.

Now in the lonely hour when with her ray
The moon o'er ocean trailed a shimmering way

That the bright Spirit-folk to heaven might take,
A voice struck Naisi's ear and bade him wake.
Sudden he woke and wondering, to behold,
Beneath the couch's furs and cloth of gold,
His wife beside him wrapt in sleep serene,
And 'mid the pillows, in the moony sheen,
His little boy with wild eyes weird and bright
Laughing and crowing loud in huge delight,
With dimpled arms outstretched all silvered o'er
By moonbeams from the calm tent's open door,
As if some god-like Presence none could see
With kindly wiles there woke his infant glee!
There Naisi looked, and filled with sudden awe
A mighty sword beside its scabbard saw
Stuck two good span-lengths in the grassy earth,
And bright as though the moon had given it birth
And cast it flashing down to where it stood
Within the tent-door, glorying in her flood
Of silver light. Then back in calm repose
The strong babe sank, and, wildered, Naisi rose

And bent above the weapon, marvelling
If mortal hand e'er forged so fair a thing.
And as with curious eyes the hero gazed
On the gold hilt that bright with diamonds blazed,
A spirit voice through his whole being ran,
That seemed to say, "The gift of Mananan!
Take it, and fear not!" Then with eager hand
He grasped the hilt, and plucked the dazzling
brand
From the soft earth, and from the tent withdrew
Into the light, and looked with wonder new
On the great blade whereon was picturèd
All shapes that live and move in Ocean's bed.
Long time he gazed upon its mimic sea,
Then whirled the weapon round full joyously
O'er his proud head in circles of bright flame
That made the night breeze whistle as it came.

He stood and paused; stole softly to the tent;
Donned his strong garb of war, and musing went

Down the smooth hill-side to the glassy sound,
And halted on the shore and gazed around
On rugged isle and smooth white-tented hill,
And moonlit shore, that lay all cold and still,
Sleeping as though they ne'er would wake again
To life and morning and the sea-lark's strain.
And, as he looked, a breeze blew on his face,
Perfumed with scents from all the lovely race
Of flowers that blossom by the windy sea, —
The fragrant pink, the wild anemone,
The armèd thistle ere its head grows old
And the winds blow its beard across the wold,
The foxglove, heather, and sweet-smelling thyme, —
Yea, all the flowers, from north to southland clime
That meet the morn with smiles, their odors sent,
With the fresh salty smell of ocean blent,
On that strange breeze that, waxing momently,
Fulfilled the hero with wild ecstasy
Of heart and brain, as though his footsteps fell
In heaven 'mid meadows of sweet asphodel!

And now, as stronger still the breeze blew by,
The sound's clear water caught the hero's eye:
Moveless it gleamed, with not one wave to show
That o'er its surface that weird breeze could blow.
Whereat great wonder filled him. To a tree,
That grew behind on the declivity
Of the green height, he turned: no motion there
Of branch or leaf;—not even his own dark hair
Was lifted by the marvellous wind. Around
Again the hero turned, and with a bound
Of his strong heart, and tingling cheeks all warm
From the fresh blood, beheld the giant form
Of a huge warrior, clad in sea-green mail,
Standing upon the shore. The flowing sail
Of a great bark appeared his cloak; the spray
That dances with the morning winds at play,
Topmost o'er all the woods on Scraba's elm,
Seemed the tall plume that waved above his helm,
While like a spire he stood, upon the sand
His long spear resting, towering from his hand

As a great larch's shaft in Ara's dell.
Silent he stood, the while his glances fell
On the Fomorian gate. A shadow vast
Betimes he seemed, wherethro' the moonbeams passed
With shimmering glow, or in his mantle caught,
Or linkèd mail, to Naisi's vision brought
Strange shifting shapes of all the things that be,
Living or dead, within the crystal sea!

Slowly he turned him round and bent his gaze
On Naisi. As the moon smiles o'er the haze
Of silvery splendor that some silent night
Of autumn robes the hill-ridge, kind and bright
The god-like Spectre smiled, till Usna's son
Felt the warm blood in tingling currents run
With rapture to the marrow of his bones.
Then with high-rising heart and prayerful tones
He spoke the Sea-god: "O thou, Mananan!
Friend of my race through many a century's span,

Since the first day their swelling sails they spread
To the light winds o'er Ocean's billowy bed! —
O mighty Sea-god! loud we call to thee
For help in this our dread extremity!
We ask thee not for valor; valor still
Is Usna's birthright, and the daring will
To do great deeds: but some strong sign of power,
Some portent for the battle's coming hour,
We ask of thee, O Patron great and kind!"

No voice replied, yet in his conscious mind
He felt these words: "Dare fortune thus and win!"
Then saw the towering Spectre striding in, —
Into the middle of the sound that lay
Calm at its lowest ebb. The shining ray
Of moonlight showed the spear then poised on
high,
And from the Spectre's hands loud whirring fly
'Gainst the Fomorian gate, until it found
The midmost plank; then with a direful sound

Door, jamb and bolt, disparted, inward fell,
Sharp thundering; as in Dargle's ancient dell,
At the weird silent hour when Mother Night
Spreads her wide wings with pulsing stars all bright
From pole to pole, brooding o'er land and sea
With matron care for her great family
Of men and beasts and birds, and things that creep,
Or swim the wave, till all are hushed in sleep,—
Amidst the lull an aged oak-tree falls,
Hoarse rumbling down the wild dell's rocky walls
With deafening crash into the torrent's bed,—
The wood, upstarting, wakens all adread,
The scared birds' flapping wings and chattering jar,
And wild beasts' howls, are heard from near and far
Throughout the dell; so rose the dreadful clang
Of the great spear against the gate, and rang
From isle to height; the camps awoke; each man
Grasped at his arms and to the muster ran,
Shouting his hostile challenge as he went!—
Then Naisi on the height his keen eyes bent

A moment; when he turned, the waters wan
Far shivering lay, the mighty Shade was gone
In silence as he came; — a monstrous wave
Upheaved its broad gray back, and murmuring drave
Along the sound from answering shore to shore,
While clear and sweet, commingling with its roar,
Came sounds of blowing conch and breathing shell,
And of all things that on the ocean swell
Follow the mariner's bark with omens glad, —
The wheeling sea-fowl and the dolphin mad
With the keen zest of life; then silence came,
And the young Dawn arose in ruby flame!

Fair cleared the morn, yet slow the hours went by
That saw the sound's clear waters rising high
To that still point between the ebb and flow,
When the soft rack of seaweed, trailing slow,
Uncertain seemed of restless ocean's will,
Whether to go or come. From isle and hill
Full many a fierce eye watched the dubious weed,
Eager, till oceanward it 'gan recede

Along the calm sound, like the food-gorged snake
That through the meadowy grass its way doth take,
Slow seeking, green and long, the forest wide.
And now the mid-day fires on either side
Upflung their curling smoke, and meal-time passed,
For many a valiant man of meals the last;
And the great sun 'gan take his downward way
To cool his burning brow in ocean's spray,
Lengthening the mountain shadows; while the sound,
Still sinking foot by foot, at twilight found
The Usnanian and Fomorian face to face
Embattled, ready for the dreadful race
Into each other's arms, whose clasp is death
Or victory.

Now the wind with stronger breath
Blew from the east great fleecy clouds that veiled
The stars and rising moon as on they sailed
Across the wide-spread heaven. The brothers now
Stood by the tent upon the green height's brow;

Naisi with face against his young wife's face,
And arms around her in a fond embrace
At parting; Ardan, Ainli, standing near,
Each leaning on his yellow-bladed spear,
Watching with bleeding heart the efforts vain
Of Deirdrè to control the cruel pain
That tore her breast. No words dark Naisi
said,
But to her brazen chair his sad wife led
Before the tent, and kissed his little son
And placed him on her lap; then one by one
Looked in his brothers' eyes with steadfast look,
That half of high-souled confidence partook,
And half anxiety for what might chance
To each and all in the fell fight. One glance,—
One yearning glance of love on child and wife,—
And he was gone.
Now for the dreadful strife.
Young Ainli took the left: the rightward wing
With hearts of fire heard Ardan's harness ring,

As to the front he strode; a moonlight beam
Fell upon Naisi's arms with sudden gleam
Before the central battle, while he gave
The word of onset. As the long reeds wave
With a great noise round Maga's glimmering meres
Before the storm's first blast, so waved the spears
Of Usna, when with loud-resounding tread
The host advanced: and as from Gaulty's head,
When from the south the thawing March winds
blow,
With loosened rocks and earth the piled-up snow
Of winter rushes into Bala's lake
With a great roar that all the hills doth shake,
So rattling loud, so thundering in their might,
Close packed they moved, and from the echoing
height
Dashed headlong in their fury. High was tost
The spray before their tall knees, as they crossed
The shallow sound; while, as the starlings rise
From the autumnal fields and shade the skies

With countless wings whirring upon the wind,
So rose the Fomor's arrows from behind
The palisade in clouds, and bit and clashed
On shield and brazen mail: yet forward dashed
The Usnanians, still unbroken, undismayed,
Till 'tween the tough ribs of the palisade
Some crossed the spear shaft with their stubborn
foes,
Some on the woven fence rained blows on blows
Of sounding battle-axe and bitter sword!
Then fast the archers and the slingers poured
Their missiles inward, till the mighty cry
Of battle tore unto the clouded sky,
Wherefrom the moon would gleam betimes and
show
The blood-stained water, and the fitful glow
Of brandished weapons and opposing shields
Along that ridge of death where no man yields,—
The dauntless heart, the coward, or the base,—
Save to the grisly King whom all must face!

Now from the leftward wing a mighty yell
On Naisi's watchful ear triumphant fell ; —
There Ainli, first to gain the foeman's pale,
Felt the light arrows smite his shield and mail;
And like a fierce young bull whose brindled flanks
The hunters gore by Lara's reedy banks
In the far wild, till with loud bellowing roar
And tail outstretched he scours along the shore,
Charging his foes, so Ainli, when the flight
Of shafts first clashed against his harness bright,
Rushed forward shouting, and confronted there —
The fence between them — grim-browed Adamair,
Lord of Hebridean isles, who muttering low
Cast a huge javelin at his youthful foe.
Nimbly young Ainli leapt aside : the spear,
Thirsting for heroes' blood, whizzed by his ear,
Glanced from a rock, and then rebounded high,
Still whizzing, half across the sound to fly
Ere in the brine it splashed. Then quick as run
The lightnings, Ainli from his shoulder spun

His brass-bound javelin with unerring hand:
High on the throat, above the golden band
That girt the Rover's neck, the brazen blade
Struck deep and onward its fell pathway made
Under the skull-base; — on the bloody bent
Clashing the hero fell, and Ainli sent
A fierce shout through the night, while all his men
With a wild yell to battle rushed again.
And Naisi heard the cry, and answer gave
With a great shout, and, forward bounding, drave
His mighty spear-head through the ponderous door,
By deft Fomorian hands replaced once more, —
Through boss and sea-worn plank, intent to slay,
Crashing, the cruel spear-head made its way,
Far piercing through a soldier's back and breast
Who stood behind, and bandied gibe and jest,
Laughing, with his compeers, — ah! knowing not
That Death oft seeketh man's securest spot,
To strike unseen! Down drooped the soldier's head,
And a grim pallor o'er his features spread,

And fast his heart poured forth its crimson tide,
And hanging on the spear impaled he died!
Then, as the shy wild deer that from the wood
Come forth to drink the streamlet's crystal flood,
And quench their eager thirst, and gambol free
Over the ferny glade, till suddenly
They hear the savage growl and furious charge
Of a huge wolf from out the forest's marge,
Away they bound with trembling limbs, — away
From the fell danger in their blind dismay;
So the Fomorian guard, struck pale with awe
When the great spear within the door they saw
Transfix their comrade, from their shelter fled
Behind the quaking bulwark. Terror led
Their flight, and winged their coward feet amain,
As Naisi with a shout plucked back again
His long spear, and the armèd corse fell down
Clattering upon the causeway. Then the stowne
Of war rose higher still; from pliant wrist
And ready hand full many a javelin hissed

Its serpent song far-darting, bucklers clanged
And harness rattled, and the bowstrings twanged
Resounding, and the arrows fell like sleet
On Blama from the storm-cloud sharp and fleet
Down whizzing; round the pale, without, within,
The thick ranks strove, and o'er the dreadful din
Fury with foamy lips and blinded eyes
Raised her harsh voice till earth and darkened
skies
And deep sea trembled!

As a captain brave
Who steers his bark through stormy wind and wave,
Naisi, now here, now there, his battle led,
And with high word and deed their valor fed
Unflagging, though the gradual rising tide
Floated full many a corse, and far was dyed
With blood-streaks of his kindred. On his ear
The tramp of a great host now drawing near
Down the wild isle there fell, and through the gloom
A broad black banner came, with many a plume

Behind it waving ; then a savage roar
Of joy arose that shook the island shore
From the Fomorian ranks. "With swooping wing
The Eagle comes! Great Talc! the King! the King!"
They cried exulting ; then a sudden trace
Of moonlight fell, and showed the dreadful face
Of the Fomorian King, as down he came,
His black hair on the wind, his eyes aflame
With cruel light; then all was dark ; the shower
Of darts fell tenfold thick, the fatal hour
Of the great Three seemed nigh. From the attack
On the right wing strong Ardan turned his back
A moment ; on the centre, Naisi's shout
Was heard in vain by his retreating rout
Of files confused ; yet on the leftward fray
Young Ainli, like the hill-cat to its prey
Clung to the palisade full stubbornly.
And now, as Naisi turned, the rising sea

Rolled inward wave by wave, and o'er his waist
Lapped at his mail-shirt, and full soon embraced
His warriors arm-pit high and stopped their flight;
And, as he yearning looked upon the height
To see his loved ones, sudden overhead
The moon shone out through parting clouds and
shed
A long bright shaft of glory, slanting down
Athwart the darkness on the hillock's crown,
Showing young Deirdrè on her brazen chair,
Holding her child aloft in her despair
And terror, that his little eyes might see
His father's death scene. Gleaming vividly
The light illumed them, then came trailing fast
Its splendor down the sloping hill, and passed
Across the sound still gleaming, and was gone;
And in that fleeting moment, even as one
Who gropes his way through midnight woods and
sees
At last some welcome light amid the trees,

Bringing new courage, Naisi's soul took fire
At sight of his belov'd ones. On the dire,
Dark ruin of his battle his keen gaze
Fell hopeful, as that sudden moonlight blaze
Flashed on the sound, and showed amid the wreck
A mast wind-torn from some great galley's deck
Slow floating towards him. Like the Trump of
Doom
Unto his startled foes rang through the gloom
His rallying shout: his warriors turned; the mast
Some poised on their strong shoulders, and the blast
Sang through their plumes, as toward the hostile
door,
With a great rush, at Naisi's word they tore,
Shouting, till like a war-ram 'gainst a wall
The great beam struck the door whose direful fall
Followed the shock like thunder. Inward poured
The Usnanians now. Out flashed the Sea-god's
sword
Flaming in Naisi's grasp, and far and near
Shrank the Fomorians, shuddering in their fear

Before him, as they saw the dreadful brand
Rising and falling in the hero's hand!

Now Ainli, Ardan's voices left and right
Like cheering trumpets echoed o'er the fight,
While fast before their charge they swept the foe;
As two converging fires, when strong winds blow
In a great wood at night, with fearful glare
Come roaring on, each wild beast from his lair
Rushing in terror, onward thundering drove
Their thick spear-bristling battles, while above,
The clouds disparting, bright the moon sailed
out
In the blue heaven, and showed the helpless rout
Of the Fomorians hedged around, and gored
By showers of shafts and javelins. Shrilly roared
The wind; again the moon hid; Mercy fled
The field despairing; Rage or coward Dread
Possessed all hearts; while, raising her wild shriek,
Slaughter with crimson wings and raven beak

Flapped the black sky above exultingly:
Till, as the sinking moon from o'er the sea
Cast her last beams ere morn across the isle,
Weirdly they glimmered on the ghastly pile
Of pirate dead that cumbered all the strand,
Whereby strong Naisi stood, in his left hand
Holding aloft the grim and gory head
Of the Fomorian King!
Now rosy red
The morn arises, and the clouds of night
From sea and glittering landscape take their
flight
Before the conquering sun; and with them go
The clouds of doubt, of terror, and of woe
From Deirdrè's mind, as on her chariot seat
She sits with Gaier, and hears the armèd feet
Tramp round her of her husband's host; while he
Walks by the car, the light of victory
Within his dark eyes drowned in love. Before
The chariot, as they gain the sunlit shore,

To cross the sound, the maids and children sing
Their songs of joy, and woven garlands fling
On the white steeds and car ; the harpers play
Their notes of triumph, while the trumpets bray
Hoarse symphony. The sound is crossed, they
gain
The ships and set their wide sails o'er the main,
And clear the bay, and with a favoring wind
Leave the wild isle and their dead foes behind,
And, steering north by east, at length they view
Slieve League's high head loom o'er the waters blue,
And thence by Arran's rocks and Torry's spray,
For Alba's friendly shores they sail away,
Rejoicing, till their long black galleys ride
Moyle's hoarse-resounding, high-wave-curling tide !

THE SOJOURN IN ALBA.

SWIFT cleaving through the midmost wave
that roars
'Tween woody Erin and fair Alba's shores,
The galleys swam, as sank the saffron light
Of the third day on ocean's bosom bright,
Shimmering along the glittering golden spray
To Ulad's windy forelands far away.
As from the north when Winter 'gins his reign,
The giant whales plough south the yielding main
In a great shoal, to reach the warmer seas
That wash wild Orkney's isles and Hebrides,—
With heads unerring pointed towards their goal,
O'er the wide waste careers the mighty shoal

Behind their King, the huge bull whale, whose track
Gleams with white spray, far furrowing ocean's
back;
So the fleet clove the billows, following
The great war galley of the conquered King,
Upon whose deck the brothers stood, while she,—
The loved one,—with her child sat smilingly
Amidst them on her carvèd brazen chair.
Over the royal deck, around them there,
Barbaric shone the trophies of the fight,—
Round-rimmed, emblazoned shields and swords of
might,
Mantles of many colors, white and green,
Saffron and blue, and scarlet's dazzling sheen,
Bales of bright silks torn by pirate hands
From the sacked towns of weeping southern lands,
Great spears bedecked with many a golden stud,
And helms and mail-shirts still unwashed of blood.

With Deirdrè sat her maids,—Fingalla fair,
And blue-eyed Aoifè of the nut-brown hair.

Lightly they laughed with many a merry wile
And prank and look to win the baby's smile,
Who danced himself upon his mother's knee
And laughed in turn, and crowed full lustily.
And Naisi, looking on them, felt the sweet
Of life make all his pulses warmly beat,
And his great heart o'erfill with thankfulness
To the Almighty Gods who, from distress
And life-long trouble and despair and moan,
Work jöy to mortals, when all hope seems gone!
Then turned the hero round, and walked full slow
Astern, wherefrom through sunset's fading glow
The far Ulidian capes he still could see
Upraise their windy foreheads. Silently
Like one adream he gazed on them the while
With yearning heart, till died the day's last smile,
And o'er the gray sea crept the silent night
With the pale moon and stars all diamond bright
Sparkling upon the waters, and the breeze
Freshened apace, and o'er the swelling seas,

Incessant, the white steeds of Mananan
Chased his black galley o'er the waters wan.

And all that night they sailed, and as they sped
Upon their right passed many a towering head
Of hill and cape and many a lonely strand
And forest of the wild Cantyrian land.
And now within the east the shining dawn
Clomb up the sky, and leafy brake and lawn,
Low-lying mead and purple highland tract,
Dell, stream, and gorge, and vapory cataract
Of the strange land, both near and far away,
Crept out of night's black shadow into day;
And the breeze lulled, and from his vermeil bed
The sun upraised his glorious, gladsome head
And looked with smile benign o'er earth and sea.
'Neath the fresh morn the Usnanians joyously
Still onward sailed, till 'tween two headlands gray
They steered into a lovely, land-locked bay,

Where on their left the mountains rose full high
From the blue water to the bluer sky,
Robed in red heath and mosses golden brown.
Far on their front, a mighty stream flung down
Its waters through the great gorge it had made
To the calm bay, in many a bright cascade,
Now lost in groves of pine, now shadowèd
By some steep crag that reared its hoary head,
Hail-hammered by the storms of centuries,
High o'er the forest. On their right, the breeze
Curled the light wavelets to the sloping strand
That lay 'tween water and the grassy land, —
Green, grassy land whereon the autumn flowers
Glittered o'er glade and lawn, as gleam the showers
Of falling stars on some far boreal sea; —
There o'er the sward the lovely rowan tree
Drooped with its clusters all vermilion red
Of berries bright, and high its tapering head
The larch uplifted, and the silver bolls
Of birches glimmered from their ferny knolls;

And the great oak-tree and the giant pine,
Girt with green ivy or the woodland vine,
Grew here and there in all their majesty;
And the dark holly shone, and gracefully
The slender ash in spots stood all alone,
Like a coy virgin. Onward, thicker grown,
Spread nut-woods, merging in a forest vast
Where red deer ranged and wild boars crunched
the mast,
And the gray wolf and savage bear abode.
Bright over all the saffron morning glowed
With genial ray that made the wild-birds sing
In that fair place and joy rule every thing.

Now on the galleys' sides the warriors' shields,
Locked rim by rim, displayed their shining fields
To the glad sun with fair emblazonery;
And o'er their glittering edges one could see
Of maids and children many a gleesome face
Look with delight upon that lovely place,

And on broad deck and poop their elders stand
In eager converse, each with pointed hand
Stretched towards green glade or dell that semblance bore
To some loved spot upon their native shore.
And, as they stood, they heard the loud command
Of Naisi ringing over sea and land,
Soon followed by the merry sailors' song,
As noisily the well-ranged fleet along
They cast the anchors and the oars drew in,
And furled the sails; then fast the joyful din
Increased and drowned the song the shipmen sung;
The children laughed, and many an old dame's tongue
Wagged voluble; the great hounds bayed, the plash
Of lowering boats was heard; the ring and clash
Of armor sounded as the warriors took
Their shields from off the bulwarks strong, and shook
Their spears with gladness. Midway to the shore
Dark Naisi's boat full fast now plied the oar,

With its lov'd freight; and as they neared the strand,
Shouting his war-shout, Ardan sprung to land,
Striding full swift the wave-washed space to pass,
And struck his spear-butt through the woven grass
Into the woodland earth, and left it there,
Its rings and broad blade shining high in air;
Then turned again unto the boat, and bore
In his strong arms young Gaier along the shore
To the green spot where towered his mighty spear.
There stood he smiling as his kin drew near,
And blithely said, "O sister! brothers mine!
Look on this lovely land, this sun benign
Laughing good omen on us from the skies!
Be sure, in after time, in goodly wise
Our kingdom here o'er all the land shall spread,
Won by our might; and when the years have fled
Prosperous for us, and we are old and gray,
This little hand the regal rod shall sway!"

Now in the pleasant afternoon the feet
Of the great tribe had pressed the grasses sweet
Of the fair sunny woodland, save of those
The shipmen left behind. The long repose
Of the sweet pleasance now seemed lost alway; —
Loud bayed the fierce hounds to the charger's neigh;
With shrilly scream the royal ger-falcon
Fluttered his wings the mail-clad wrist upon,
Glad at the woodland sights; the cheery sound
Of mallets echoed, in the thymy ground
Driving the tent-pegs; while from tree to tree
The children played and shouted joyfully.
Whereat an ancient raven who had seen
Long centuries within that woodland green,
By man untroubled, on his aged oak
From his sweet noontide slumber now awoke
And shook himself, and slowly 'gan to draw
Across his reverend head his wrinkled claw,
And winked his wise old eyes, and looking out
Through the thin branches saw the joyous rout

With all its social sounds; then suddenly
He spread his wings, far, far away to flee
In dudgeon dire to other woods remote!

There, ere the winter winds the hillside smote,
They built their mighty dun, with earthen mound
And watery ditch tri-circled round and round,
Strong-gated and compact; and with great toil
Therein they gathered all the woodland spoil:
Fish, with their trawling nets spread long and wide
They reft in myriads from the teeming tide
Of sea and stream; and deftly did they take
The fowl in many a flock from wood and lake;
They slew the brown bear in his forest hoar,
Within his nut-strewn wood the savage boar,
And out on mountain sides and moorlands brown
The dun bull and his herd they hunted down
With food-providing spears; while hawk and hound
Made joyous tumult through the wildwoods round,

Chasing the heron and far-bounding deer
To sound of horn and huntsman's merry cheer.

And now hoar Winter, where the friendly Star
That guides the wandering galley shines afar
In the bright zenith fixt, his storehouse vast
Of feathery crystals opened; and the blast
That guards the Pole, let loose, his pinions light
Spread out wide winnowing one silent night
O'er isle and continent the pearly snow,
Till morning rose, and solemnly and slow
The great flakes still fell down. Within the dun
The gleeful children round began to run,
And clapped their little hands and cried, "The geese!
The wild geese shed their feathers!" fleece on fleece
Of the soft floss falling upon their play,—
And falling, falling all the livelong day
And all the night till the next morning came,
And for the first time, gay with golden flame,

The sun arose unwelcomed by the bills
Of tuneful birds or sounds of murmuring rills.

Within her chamber sat the mother fair,
Her loved ones by her, as the stilly air
Of that calm day was darkening into night;
And ne'er on looks more gladsome fell the light
Of lamp, or ruddy fire of hearth, than theirs.
And well forgotten now seemed all their cares, —
So well, that in the warm and social gleam
Of the bright fire the embers 'gan to seem
To each glad eye arranged in castles gay,
And landscapes of delight where life's young
May
Was all calm sunshine and fair blossoming,
Untouched by past or future's bitter sting!
And yet, 'mongst all the brightness, still there lay
A shadow upon Deirdrè's soul, whose sway
Showed its fell presence, though infrequently,
In this wise: once her child upon her knee

She took from Aoifè's arms, and placed her
hand
On his young noble head, and curious scanned
His eyes, as though she sought to find therein
Some impress of the Doom of death and sin
By Caffa prophesied ; and finding nought
But life and laughter, inward turned her thought,
As if communing with the Gods awhile ;
Then looked again and met the infant's smile,
And bent her down and kissed him silently,
And murmured to herself, "'Twixt Them and me
I place thee, O my babe!"
And now she took
Her husband's hand, and with a joyful look
Said, "Here perchance our days may all be glad!—
In the world's life are mixed the Good, the Bad,
For man's own choosing, and who chooseth well
Wins happiness. O love, what tongue can tell
The dangers thou hast conquered to attain
This haven of our rest from fear and pain?

Then steadfast keep thy mind to tempt no more
New dangers, and upon this friendly shore
Our lives may pass, and love triumphant be
O'er the King's wrath and Caffa's prophecy!"

Then Naisi smiled, and, "Fear not, love!" he said.
"No weakly tribe were we when sore bested,
Nor feebler now in peace to hold our own
In this strange land, than our sires dead and gone,
Whose valiant maxim was, through great and small,
'Fight Danger on his own side of the wall!'"
With hand still clasped in hers, "O peerless one!"
He cried again, "look on thy little son.
May the Gods calm through him thy strange alarm,
And with his infant wiles thy soul so charm
To happiness, that thou may'st all forget
Thy boding fears; though never spok'st thou yet
But that some Godhead utterance seemed to find
From thy sweet mouth. O best of womankind,

Well sayest thou Good is gain, and Evil loss,
And wild Ambition's fruit but bitter dross,
And Love the flower of life, the priceless gift
The Gods the brave bestow whose swords are swift
To guard it, and whose hearts Adversity
Can conquer not, nor fire, air, earth, or sea,
Divide from the belov'd!"

Now brooding came
Night's wings on earth inwrought with starry flame,
And round the Dun hushed every sound, save those
That from the merry banquet-hall arose.
Round the fair chamber all had gathered there,
Rury the Bard to hear, whose silvered hair,
Thrown back, displayed his forehead broad and white
High-domed above his rapt eyes jewel-bright,
And noble face and flowing beard of snow.
With the six royal colors all aglow
His ample garments shone, as preluding
His epic song, he touched the sounding string.

Usna's Arch Bard was he. And first he sang
The Song of Conquest: how the island rang
With sound of warring storms and demon cries,
And magic thunders bellowing through the skies;
And how the Three Seas donned their robes of mist
Made by the Danaans, and how roared and hissed
The huge waves, heaved aloft to hide the coast
From Miled's sons and the Milesian host
With unavailing clamor; how the fray
Raged by the southern shore the livelong day;
How Fas the Fair was slain, and how she died
Who sleeps within the cool glen by the side
Of the gray sea, — Scota the Flower-bright Queen,
Whose lonely grave in summer sparkles sheen
With many a fragrant blossom in that dell
Of wild Sleemis the Windy; and how fell
'Neath the Milesian spears in Tailti's fight
The regal sons of Kermad, and the might
Of Miled's seed won Erin's sovereignty,
From Toth's loud wave to Cleena's murmuring sea!

And thus each night he sang some ancient lay,
And thus within the Dun time passed away
Till three moons waned and all the snows were
gone,
And velvet catkins on the willow shone
By lowland streams, and on the hills the larch
Scented with odorous buds the winds of March.

One glimpse of Spring to pass away too soon!—
Out from the iron East, one afternoon,
A wind arose full chilly, and began
With blighting breath the tender twigs to fan,
And through the pine woods make its bitter moan,
With power each day waxed stronger, as if blown
From the fell mouth of fast-pursuing Fate,
Continuous, till the groves were desolate,
And hill and dale, of every living thing,
And tender bud and blossom of the spring.
And now the chase no more its guerdon gave,
And as the wildwood barren was the wave,

While blew that poisoned breeze; and cheeks grew
white
Within the Dun, for Hunger there 'gan bite
The tribe with bitter fangs. Then one drear day
With five score champions Naisi strode away
Eastward along the hillsides, with the sword
To win them food. As troops a savage horde
Of wolves in winter, questing for their prey
O'er the low plains from Crotta's mountains gray
With gnashing teeth and wild red roving eyes,
So stalked they forth. Within the leaden skies
The sun sank cheerless, and with wannish flame
Arose next morn, but still no tidings came
Of the bold absent ones.

"O brother brave,"
Then Ardan cried to Ainli, "by what wave,
Or wood, or hill, or town of this strange land,
Doth Naisi lift the long spear in his hand
And show the golden Osprey on his shield?
Perchance, full hard bested on fell or field,

O'er the bright orb he fearless eyes the foe,
In war's hot barter changing blow for blow.
Go thou and find, and aid him at his need."

Joyful young Ainli donned his warlike weed
Of bull-hide strong, well fenced with scales of
brass,
And striding fierce went through the eastern pass,
And showed the Hill Cat gleaming on the boss
Of his broad shield o'er many a moor and moss,
Followed by four score champions. From the height
Over the bay came down the gloomy night,
Her ancient plumes by kindly dews unwet;
And morning rose, but brought no tidings yet
To Ardan, who, ere noon, with three score men
Brass-panoplied marched through the eastern glen
Grimly and stern. Full many a hill and wold
Saw the great fighting Boar of graven gold
Glittering upon his shield as he went on,
Till on his broad strong back the evening sun

Glanced red against the buff-coat's brazen scales,
And from a shaggy height that o'er the vales
Rose towering, he looked down and saw a sight
That filled his valiant heart with fierce delight.

Beneath him, scarce an arrow flight away,
Fenced round by rocks and trees, a hollow lay,
With one rough outlet, steep, of narrow span,
Wherethro' in foam a shallow torrent ran
With bickering voice. Now o'er the torrent's bed
And the small path that by its waters led
From th' outward plain, with loud-resounding din
A mighty herd of kine came driving in,
Filling the hollow. High the steam arose
From their perspiring backs, like that which shows
Its rolling mists at morn o'er Gada's mere
Amid the young spring meadows, when the year
Dries its last hoar-frost in the risen sun
And dim-seen cattle round the pastures run!
Up the rough narrow pathway, like the wind

Strode Naisi's men, the maddened rout behind;
While he, three full rods at their rearward, came
With haughty front and threatening eye of flame,
Turning betimes upon the foe that pressed
Close on his footsteps, o'er his mighty breast
His shield upraised, and by his towering head
His huge spear poised with blade all purple red
From the fresh gore it spilt; so turns the bear
Whom hunters fighting follow to his lair
With deafening clamor up some desert pass
Where Sulitelma rears its snow-white mass
High o'er Norwegian woods; — vengeful he turns,
While the hot wrath within his red eye burns,
And furious rends with cruel teeth and claw
And savage growl the foes that nigh him draw!

And now the hollow's widening sward they gain,
And Naisi, turning, halts and shouts amain
Unto his warriors, who come rushing back
With levelled spears to guard the narrow track;

And the foe halts, and their thick press divides,
Like waves around a war-ship's shining sides,
While from the rearward, on a huge black steed
In barbarous trappings dight, with headlong speed
Loud clanging, rode a warrior grim and old,
Large-limbed, and clad in gleaming weed of gold
And brass and burnished steel: with blazing eye
He checked his steed and raised his spear on
high,
And looked on Naisi full of wrath and pride,
And in a voice of thunder thus he cried: —

"Dog of a stranger! whence art thou? and where,
In this our country, buildest thou thy lair?
What thief of thieves begat thee? Art thou dumb?
Speak ere thou diest, for thine hour is come!
Ha! hear the wild cat's cry from yonder wood
With hungry clamor calling for thy blood,
And from the hill the grumbling of the boar
That soon shall dip his sharp tusks in thy gore!"

Then Naisi, hearkening, heard the signal cry,—
Hill Cat and Boar,—and knew his brothers nigh,
And at the old man shook his spear and said,—
'Ha! likelier shall their hungry maws be fed
With flesh of thee and thine, for I am one
Whom men call Naisi, mighty Usna's son,
From Erin's northern coast. I asked for food
With kindly words from these thy followers
rude,
And got but ribald speech, old man, like thine!
For them and thee the wives and maids shall pine
Of this thine Alban land; the Osprey's beak
The heart's blood in thy riven breast shall seek;
For, hark! the Wild Cat's cry draws nearer still,
And mighty Boar-Shield rushes down the hill!"
He said, and, as on high his weapon shone,
Cried, "Ware the Osprey's swoop!" and then fell
on.
And scarce the whizzing spear had left his hand,
When from the ambush Ainli with his band

Rushed from the wood, and Ardan fierce and strong
At the same moment joined the struggling throng,
That for a dreadful space swayed to and fro,
In desperate conflict mixed, till far below
The stream-bed seemed as if the tumbling flood
Had torn from out its roots some wintry wood,
And swept it downward with resounding roar,
Choking its gorge and tearing all its shore
With tossing trunk and branch and flickering spray;
So raged between the cliffs the clamorous fray,
Close packed and joined in one great whelming wave
Of struggling men and bickering spear and glaive!

Sharp was the onset, short the battle roared:
The foe went down before the Usnanian sword;
The foaming torrent ran with bloody stain,
The vanquished fled, the victors spoiled the slain,
And no fierce captives took save him alone,
Aran, the aged chief of high Dunthrone,

Whom Naisi tore from off his snorting steed
'Mid the thick battle press. Then with the speed
Of a wild wind of March they swept away
Through the rough glens, exulting, with their
prey,
And reached the Dun as the first beams of morn
Rose in the east and lit the hills forlorn.

Great was the triumph, loud the mirth and glee,
Within the Dun that gallant sight to see;
Out to the gate came Deirdrè with her boy,
And in her husband's arms returning joy
Sparkled within her eyes of heavenly blue,
And to her cheeks restored the roses' hue.
And, as around the throng her glances ran,
With pity fell they on the grim old man,
Aran the captive, in his golden dress
Now soiled and rent from out the battle press.
No drooping captive he: haughty he stood,
Straight as a pine stem in Glenara's wood;

Yet, as he met her glance, the hostile glare
Left his fierce eyes and a kind look came there;
And turning unto Naisi wonderingly,—
"Now, by the Gods!" he cried, "what men be ye,
Who, while this night my bitter tongue did burn
With words of rage, gave kind ones in return?
Whose women, like this peerless wife of thine,
Look on my hapless state with eyes benign?
Why slay me not? as erst by Solway's shore
I slew the Roman knight this hauberk wore,
And spoiled him of his golden finery
Even when the fight was won; for I am he,
Aran of high Dunthrone, whose northern blade
In Rome's firm ranks the first red havoc made,
When by my side our King, now tall and strong
As thou art, then a stripling, all day long
Fought with his hand lashed to the sword's bright hilt,
Fearing to lose his grasp; and redly gilt

Were hand and sword ere ending of that field,
For well I taught him 'neath the Roman shield
To plant his steel within the Roman heart.
Then slay me! slay! and let my soul depart
Unto the mighty Gods who love the brave,
Rather than live in bonds and die a slave!"

"No slave art thou!" said Naisi: "we were taught
Reverence for age and valor. Dearly bought
The knowledge comes to youth that with it brings
Contempt for such as thou. In all fair things
Our guest thou art: or now even thou art free
To go back to thy King, whoe'er he be!"

Great feast they made: the fat flesh of the spoil
On spits did smoke, in brazen cauldrons boil,
And a sweet steam arose, and red wine flowed
Till the third morning o'er the mountains glowed.
Then from their ships a coat of mail they brought
With bright brass blazing and with gold inwrought,

A hawk, a hound, a war-horse snowy-white
With golden selle and purple trappings dight,
A royal brooch, a cloak of scarlet fold,
A broad-orbed shield rimmed round with graven
gold,
A sword with many a jewel glittering,
And sent them as a peace-gift to the King,
With the old chief, who, as he rode away,
Still dubious said, "What kind of men be they?"

The days went on: soft sunny showers of rain
Sprinkled the barren ridge and parchèd plain,
And wild flowers oped their lovely painted bells,
And grass grew green, and birds sang in the dells,
And all was glad when the ninth morning burned
Over the hills, and the old lord returned
With many a gift, and message kind to come
To the King's house and find therein a home.

Then Naisi left the fourth part of his host
Ward over fleet and Dun, and from the coast

Moved inland three days' march, and ere the night
Of the third day camped 'neath a woody height
In a green dell, wherethro' a murmuring stream
Ran with its bordering meadows all agleam
With new-sprung vernal flowers. Then Deirdrè
said:
"By some fair-seeming fortune we are led,
O Naisi, through this land; but take thou heed
Where want of foresight or mishap may lead.
This wild King hath no wife: some day perchance
My luckless face may meet his ardent glance,
And danger follow, O fond love, to thee,
And parting from thine arms and death to me!
Then reach his town beneath the night's dark shade,
And 'neath the darkness be our campment made,
And in the tents conceal us women all,
Ere thou goest up unto the great King's hall."

And so 'twas done. One day's march lay between
The King's fair palace and that woodland green;

And, as the next night's darkness gathered
down,
They pitched their camp outside the royal town.
Then morning's splendor came; and Naisi rose,
And with his brothers ten stout warriors chose,
Armed as for battle, for his following,
And left his tents and went before the King.

Now young this King was, as old Aran said;
Impulsive, proud and brave, and still unwed;
And, trained since childhood 'mid the clash of spears,
Was wise in war, though scarce of Naisi's years.
Handsome he was, and knit in giant mould;
Broad were his brows; his hair, like swarthy gold,
From its bright circlet fell with tawny stain
O'er his strong shoulders like a lion's mane;
Haughty the look within his large gray eye
As the young eagle's on the mountain high;
Rich were the robes he wore with kingly grace;
And like a ruddy morning was his face.

And now, as 'mid his armèd nobles all,
He saw the Usnanians striding up the hall,
His bold brow flushed a little, and the sheen
Of valor in his eye grew warm and keen,
As though some quick thought swelled his heart
with pride
Of great deeds yet with them done side by side,
On fields where young men mighty of their hands
Love the wild war-shout and the clash of brands.
Graceful he rose, and on his royal chair
Placed his strong hand and paused a moment
there,
Till glittering bright before him Naisi stood
With his tall band.
"O rover of the wood,
That knowest so well," he said, "to rob and slay
In this our realm, now what hast thou to say?"

He smiled, yet at the question Naisi's eye
Sparkled full stern before he made reply,

"But this," he answered: "place thine enemies,
O King, before us, and the self-same breeze
That fans thy banner let it blow on ours;
And be they Roman ranks, or Northern powers,
That face us, we will give, as best we can,
Five score to feed thy wolves for every man
We slew of thine; and, as a token sure,
Take thou mine hand, that friendship may endure
Between us while the heart of Honor beats!"

Bright the King smiled, and said, "The hand that meets
Thine other than in friendship firm must be,
And doubly armed against adversity;
And thus I take thine hand, and thus I say,
Well met, O comrade, on this lucky day!"

Now scarce the April moon's pale light had gone,
When in the sun the warlike banners shone

Of King and prince; and many a battle tide
With conquering swords the twain stemmed side by side,
Each well-fought field but adding strength the more
To the hot friendship each the other bore,
Till one full year had passed in joy away,
And fields were white with daisies of the May.

It chanced upon a morn of early spring,
When flowers began to bloom and birds to sing,
That Starn, the royal Steward, passing by
The camp of Usna, cast his prying eye
On Deirdrè, as she sat beneath a tree
Outside her tent door. Long and curiously
He eyed her from the grove wherein he stood,
Then walked away in silent gladsome mood,
Like one who by a lucky chance hath found
Some treasure rare long hidden underground.
Yet said he nought until the King came home
From hostile shores washed by the North Sea's foam,

Where he and his and Usna's host imbrued
Their spears in blood, and many a tribe subdued.
Then went he to the King.
"Now by thy head!
And by my father's hand, O King!" he said,
"The gem of gems I've found thee. I have seen
In Usna's camp bright Beauty's peerless queen,
The wife of Naisi, — beautiful beyond
All youth's imaginings or day-dreams fond, —
Yea! yea! so beautiful that I — even I —
Stood for a moment in wild ecstasy
And blessed the Gods that made her! Take her then
Unto thy throne, and slay these stranger men
In open hall, or bid me privately
To slay them!"
But the King said, "Far from me,
O Starn! be that fell day when Friendship's band
And Honor's law I break with mine own hand.
Then tempt me not."

But Starn said, "Though the blood
Within thy heart from childhood frozen stood,
'Twould melt, O King, before her face divine,
And run through all thy veins like boiling wine!
But go thyself. Watch from the grove and see,
Then try and measure what thy love shall be!"

And the King sought the grove himself, and saw;
And Friendship's sacred tie and Honor's law,
And fear and shame, and sense of wrong and right,
Fled from his maddened bosom at the sight,
And in their stead there burned a raging flame
Of blindfold love no power on earth could tame.
"O Starn," he said, "go seek her privily,
And promise all a queen should have from me!"

One morn while King and prince a hosting made
Far in the west; while every grove and glade
Around the camp with fragrant bloom was bright
Of daisies, primroses, and shamrocks white,

And hyacinths that with their trembling bells
Like a blue robe from heaven shone down the
dells,
Twinkling with diamond dew-drops,—to the screen
Of the sweet grove the old man came unseen,
And looked, and by the tent found Deirdrè there,
Sitting and weaving flowers in garlands fair
To crown her little boy, who on her knee
Laughed in the dancing shadows of the tree
That o'er them spread, rustling with young birds'
wings.

"Sweet is the song each bird of beauty sings
To him that owns it," Starn thought, as he came
Out from the grove and told his tale of shame
And purpose dread. Then rose the loyal wife,
Grasping her babe full firm.
"Now, by thy life,
O aged dog!" she cried, "come here no more!
Thy little King! Upon our native shore

The true hand of a King worth ten like thine
I cast away for this brave lord of mine!
Begone! and leave me to my thoughts alone!"
He fled, and sinking down she made her moan,
Clasping her child and rocking to and fro
In trembling fear and new-awakened woe!

Four days before the Baeltin Feast, at noon
The hosts returned in triumph, and full soon
Went Starn unto the King and told his tale,
Whereat the monarch's brow with wrath grew pale,
And ten times stronger his hot bosom strove
With thoughts of vengeance and unlawful love.
And fierce he cried:
"O Starn, come woe or weal,
Usna shall fall beneath the Alban steel
Before to-morrow's light!"
"Nay, nay, O King!"
Old Starn replied. "The Baeltin feast will bring

The hour to slay them, when unguardedly
They sit around the board and in their glee
Quaff the red wine within thy royal hall:
Then let them feel the Alban sword and fall,
Else, by the Gods! full stern shall be the fight
Ere they are slain!"

But on that very night,
When Naisi knew the Alban's treacherous mind,
He struck his camp, and left the town behind
Full many a mile ere rose the morning ray,
As westward to his fleet he made his way.
Three days they marched in thunder, for they knew
No safety now but o'er the ocean blue
To spread their sails and seek another coast
Would shield them from the King's pursuing host;
And on the third day, at the evening hour,
With thankful hearts beheld the mountains tower
Over the friendly bay, that on its breast
Painted each precipice from foot to crest;

They saw their numerous galleys side by side
Ranged in fair order on the glassy tide,
The groves, the gorge, the gleaming torrent run,
The bloom-bright woodland, and the smoking Dun
Wherein full many a festal fire did burn.
Glad was the shout that welcomed their return
From that part of the host with forethought meet
They left behind to guard both Dun and fleet,
And who from shore and wood came thronging now
Round the strong gate with many a leafy bough;
For this was Baeltin Eve, and brakes and bowers,
Copses and dells, were ransacked of their flowers
To deck the morrow's feast. Each gate and door
With garlands and green leaves was covered o'er;
And Naisi smiled with pleasure and amaze
When on his marshalled fleet he turned his gaze,
For there the hulls that erst were black as night
Now shone, with many an image strange bedight,
Limned in barbaric sheen of cinnabar,
And purple rich from Roman lands afar,

And from the swarthy Orient red and blue,
Primeval woad, and many another hue
Of pigments by the sailors found amid
The huge heaps of Fomorian booty hid.
Above the fleet three giant galleys rose:
Midmost Talc's mighty war-ship, and of those, —
The other twain, — one to the leftward lay,
One flaunted o'er the right its pennons gay.
Over the wave, each lofty prow upon,
Well carved and gilt, a figure-head there shone,
Made by the tribe's artificers: the left
Bore the great Hill Cat wrought with fingers deft,
Holding a silver salmon in his claw,
Young Ainli's cognizance; with open jaw,
And gleaming tusks and shaggy breast of might,
And bristling back, the Wild Boar on the right
Seemed charging sheer into the dolphin's bath;
And on the King's ship th' Osprey in his wrath
Swooped on his quarry from the cloudy height;
While like some Orient grove with blossoms bright

Of climbers' dazzling glories, wide outspread
From mast and spar, the fleet was garlanded
With sprays of green, and flowers from wood and lea,
Culled by glad hands, to grace the revelry
And games of that great Feast of bloom and mirth
That welcomed summer to the songful earth!

That night, with sharpened sense and watchful ear,
Brave Naisi slept, and morn rose calm and clear,
And the first Baelfire, lit, its tongues of flame
Tossed upward towards the bright sun whence it came;
When, all at once, a scout in headlong speed
Dashed from the east upon his foaming steed
Into the Dun, and told how through the wood,
Three leagues off, Aran came, athirst for blood,
With a great host pursuing. Wrathfully
The brothers grasped their spears, and to the sea

Betook them with their mighty tribe again;
And scarce on deck the last band of their men
Had sprung with clashing harness, when the shore
And all the wood shook with the loud uproar
Made by the Alban host now drawing nigh
In long-spread rushing ranks ; so, when the sky
And wallowing sea are mixed in cloud and spray
By the wild storm upon some wintry day,
The fast high-curling surges roll amain,
Each following each, to flood the sandy plain
Of windy Rossapenna in the north!

And now from out his ranks came Aran forth,
And laughed a bitter laugh, and from the strand
At the Usnanians shook his armèd hand,
And like a trumpet cried: —

"O small-souled men!
With valor like the little water-hen,
That at the otter's plunge scuds o'er the wave
To hide its head within some reedy cave

Under the stream-bank, till the danger's o'er,—
Why leave ye in such haste this pleasant shore
Like churls, with your unfought-for, glorious prize?
Bethink ye! Better is his fate who dies
On the brave war-field, than of those who crawl
Unto their beds, and turning to the wall,
Racking in pains and writhing in despair,
Inglorious, give their base souls to the air!
Come forth then from your ships, for vain do ye
Now seek for safety on the windy sea!
There rides our valiant King with all his fleet.
Come forth then! Better on this woodland meet
The brunt of war, treading the pleasant grass,
Than meet the King and through the cold door
pass
Of Death, to feed the dwellers of the wave!
Come forth and fight!"

"Enough and more we gave,
O vain old man, to thee in yonder wood
Of fight before!" cried Naisi, as he stood

High on the Osprey's poop. "Enough and more,
Whilst thou stand'st watching vainly on the shore,
Thy King shall get within this very bay!
For see! Between the capes his pennons play,
In the wind's teeth advanced a goodly span.
Now mark thou well thy monarch's fate, old man,
Meeting the bitter edge of Usna's steel
With other hands than friendly!"
Like the peal
Of the loud clarion ere the valiant cross
Their bickering swords with shields faced boss to boss
On the red field of war, from left to right
Of the long fleet rang Naisi's voice of might,
Ordering his battle. Loud the capstan's groan
Shipping the anchors; strong the broad sails blown
Swelled their white bellies to the sunny ray;
Out flew the oars, to wreaths of hissing spray
Churning the waters with well-measured sweep;
And the fleet moved, first slowly, on the deep,

Till gathering strength at last along the main
It swept, far furrowing all the watery plain!

And now, as at the morn from Ennel's lake
In a great flock the whirring wild-fowl break,
And first confused climb up the brightening sky,
Then in a long line range themselves on high,
With sounding wings stemming the ether blue;
So the Albanian fleet together drew
Embattled from the far-off gleaming strait,
Swift moving up to meet the doubtful fate
Of combat on the unstable waste of brine;
While, on the other side, the Usnanian line
Swept toward them, till a well-flung javelin cast
Might count the space 'tween hostile mast and mast.
Then both sides paused, with back-swept careful oar;
And from the King's poop, like the wild-bull's roar,
Rang his strong voice:—

"Thou seek'st an early grave,
Usnanian, 'neath the ocean's boiling wave,
Fronting me thus; though, by the Gods! I know
Thou yieldest not without a manful blow,
With high heart caring nought for death or life!
Then take thou this, first messenger of strife
Between us!"
As he said, he raised on high
His mighty hand and made his javelin fly
Shrill whizzing, till it struck the broad-orbed shield
Of Naisi nigh the midmost of its field
With a great clang, and humming glanced aside
And in the mast stuck quivering. In his pride
Of wrath and strength rushing upon his prey,
The shaggy north bear roars; so on that day
With rage fierce Naisi shouted, as he cast
His dreadful spear, that like the lightning passed
And struck the King's shield where the rim of gold
Circled the boss; a third of disc and fold

Riving away in its destructive flight;
Yet, still advanced, the remnant no less bright
Of the huge shield shone o'er the King's broad
breast,
Than, sinking slow by Skellig-Mihil's crest,
Glares the great gibbous moon on Cleena's main,
When the cloud-scudding night is on the wane!

And now Rage found a voice, and either side
Thundered together: as when Wind and Tide
In adverse battle join, one furious sweeps
The Lammas floods from Blooma's far-off steeps
Down Shamon's bed: one drives with deafening roar
'Tween old Canlemy's Rock and Kerry's shore
The boiling ocean in; with high-raised back,
Spray-brindled, huge, comes on each watery wrack,
Meeting from strand to strand, in chaos dread
Wide wallowing, while the flashing clouds o'erhead
Thunder, and downward shoots the hissing sleet;
So on the swirling brine each hostile fleet

In giant conflict wrestled! For a space
With many a sharpened hook in fell embrace
Each galley clasped the other; yard and shroud
And prow and poop shot forth its deadly cloud
Of darts and arrows, while in hands of might
Over the bulwarks crossed the sword-blades bright,
And the plume dropped from cloven helm and crest,
And the long spear in many a valiant breast
Buried its brazen head. Ploughing the wave
'Gainst a strong Alban ship, the Wild Boar drave
Upon the right, fast as the fatal stone
From the sling whistles by a strong arm thrown;
And, as she neared the foe, at Ardan's call
With backward rush his champions one and all
Crowded the stern, that, sinking with their weight,
Heaved high the keel, while with a shout elate
The sailors strained at one tremendous sweep
Of their strong oars, and half-way from the deep
The Wild Boar sprang, and with a mighty stowne
High prow and sharpened keel went crashing down

Upon the foeman's deck, that sank beneath
With all its struggling crew, who scarce a breath
Three times from out their laboring breasts could
draw,
When the waves closed, and Ocean's ravenous maw
Swallowed them, and ne'er gave them forth again!

Loud o'er the clash of ships and cries of men
Rose the great shout of Naisi, as he stood
High on his poop, while round him, like a wood
Of larch in Bierna shaken by the blasts,
Gathered from either side the tossing masts,
And with the King's his ship came beam to beam
Resounding, and amid the clanging stream
Of missiles sharp he caught the King's fierce eye
Glaring upon him. With another cry
Of wrath, he cast his spear, and ne'er again
The brave King's foot had pressed his native plain,
Save that an arrow stronger than the rest
Of the fell shower clashed against Naisi's breast,

And glancing, th' upraised arm unerring hit,
And through the brass and leathern harness bit,
Tearing the skin small space, enough to cast
From its true aim the spear that sounding passed
By the King's side and pierced a warrior through.

And now the King's great galley backward drew,
Swift swinging round with oars again outspread
To bring on th' Osprey's beam her armèd head.
Swung round, she stops, and then returns once
more
With speed redoubling 'neath the powerful oar,
Cleaving the water in her dreadful race
'Gainst th' Osprey, that, all crowded, found no space
For turning from the shock that ne'er was given;
For like the lightning bolt that shoots from heaven
And rends some lordly castle with its flame,
Round from the left the Hill Cat plunging came,
And struck the Alban galley where the side
Bends like a shoulder forward o'er the tide,

And reft her groaning ribs in thunder, then
Backed with wide-sweeping oars to plunge again!
Needless, for through the breach the waters poured,
And 'mid the galley's hollow entrails roared;
From side to side she rocked; with dreadful yell
Flat on the broad deck many a brave man fell,
Or at the bulwark clutched full desperately,
Or from the yards plunged headlong in the sea.
Yet still the King stood calm and undismayed,
His hand upon the poop-rail as he swayed
From side to side, now low, now rising high,
Now to the Osprey's bulwark drawing nigh,
As the breach sucked the roaring waters in.
Then what in Naisi's bosom did begin
To warm it, but the brave can ever know.
With pitying eye he saw his helpless foe,
And bounded to the deck with sounding clang,
And thence upon the armèd bulwark sprang,
Grasping the shroud, and waited steadily,
Till with another roar the savage sea

Filled high the ship, that, swaying towards him,
brought
Within his generous grasp the prize he sought,—
The King, who felt as by a giant torn
From the fast lowering poop, and instant borne
Over the Osprey's bulwark, snatched away
From death, for downward through the roaring
spray
His ship plunged headlong, sunk before his eyes,
'Mid wrack and ruin and despairing cries!

Thus ceased the fight. Back to the woodland
plain
And his great host they sent the King again;
And there the fierce old lord of strong Dunthrone
Swore, by the Gods, a death of grief and moan,
With maladies unheard of, 'mid the scorn
Of men might smite him on his bed some morn,
Long lingering, if he blamed the King! "No eye
Could look on her unmoved to win or die.

And whereso'er," he said, "they wandering go,
War's fires shall burn and valiant blood shall flow
For love of her bright eyes and beauty rare!"

Meanwhile, with banners flaunting in the air,
The Usnanian fleet sailed out beyond the bay
'Tween the two looming capes, and all that day,
O'er ocean's billowy back, and all that night,
Joyful they sped, till at the morning bright
With saffron glory came they to an isle
Whereon eternal summer seemed to smile.
A heaven it looked, with purple-shining hills,
Sky-mirroring lakes, and ever-murmuring rills,
And flowery meads waved by the west wind's fan,
And shady woods wherethro' the wild deer ran,
And grass-green dells and valleys, all day long
Vocal with hum of bees and wild-birds' song.
And there they anchored in a sheltered cove,
And there beside a green leaf-whispering grove
They pitched their tents, and lived full joyously
While five years' moons waned o'er the silver sea.

THE RETURN TO EMAN.

A FEAST in Eman. Many a noble guest,
Poet and sage and hero of the best,
Sat round the glittering table with the king,
And heard the tympan and the sweet harp ring.
And to the minstrel's music, ruby-red,
The bright wine sparkled, and the mead-horn sped
From hand to hand, and laughter rose, and Care,
Queller of joy, showed no black visage there.
There sat the king, to each one bland and kind,
Yet still revolving in his secret mind
Great thoughts of doom and vengeance ; for the dart
Of Jealousy still burned within his heart
With smouldering sting, that showed no outward trace
Of its fell working on his royal face.

And there sat Conal Carna, he whose power
Swayed o'er the lands where high Dunseverick's
tower,
Perched like an osprey, in its strength and pride
Watched o'er the wave of Toth; and by his
side,
Resplendent in his youthful bravery,
Strongest of Scotic warriors, sat he,
All-beautiful Cuhullin, whose dread sword
In after-time for Eman kept the Ford
'Gainst Mab and Olild till the succor came;
And who on red Murtheimnè's field of fame
Fell in his young bloom, fighting for his land.
There Fergus Royson, at the king's right hand,
Sat smiling in his lordly raiment bright
On the glad feast, though oft another light
Filled his dark eyes of love's sweet wistfulness
At thought of some dear wile or fond caress
Of Nessa, his belov'd one, for whose smile
He bartered Eman's throne; and all the while,

Mixed with the elders' converse, one could hear
The laughter of the young knights loud and clear
Round the gay, glittering board : for all were there
Who on their golden shields the Red Branch bare.
And now the bards and minstrels, one by one,
Sang the king's praise, — fair Nessa's glorious son, —
And traced his tree generic, shaft and root,
Sweet-blossomed branch and earth-enlivening fruit,
From Miled's seed. Till 'mid the merriment
Up rose the King, and through the great hall sent
His regal voice : —
"O noble knights!" he said,
"Know ye, in all earth's kingdoms wide outspread,
A kingdom like to mine, a mansion bright
As this is in all things that with delight
O'erfill the heart? Ye know not! Ah! but yet
Think ye no thoughts betimes of sad regret
For what ye name not, that, if won, would bless
Your lives with joy, your joy with perfectness?

No! Then the Gods have made you so that nought
Humane within your hard hearts they have wrought,
Forgetful of your comrades; and must I,
Your king and lord, alone remembering sigh
O'er joys of days long past, and know ye not
Of the fair sunshine of our lives the blot
That stains it, and makes nought our happiness?
Alas! that, like a ship in sore distress,
With rudder gone and ballast spent, our state
Unsteady sails beneath the blasts of Fate,
While they are absent, — they the valiant ones,
The heroes three, great Usna's glorious sons,
And Eman's mainstay, when grim Danger's eye
Glares 'neath his black brows on us threateningly!"

Then Conal Carna answered, "Dared we say
Our rede, O King, before this happy day,
Oft had we said it; for full well we know
No hearts more brave than theirs the earth can show,

Our kindred banished. Mighty props they are
Of safety, when the fire of Bava's star
Shines lurid on the thick-hedged spears; and
well,
Ere this, the Alban king the weight can tell
Of their strong hands of valor: would thȧt they,
O King, were here to grace our revel gay!"

Then red-haired Buinè whispered mockingly,
"Behold, O brother Illan, how the sea,
With all its foe-dividing waves, can make
Love between hearts that ever longed to slake
Their vengeance in the war-tide's bloody stream!
Better for them, the Usnanians, that the beam
Of the cold polar sun should on them fall
For ever, than that they anigh this hall
Should bide one hour!"

"Nay, nay," said Illan, "nay.
What if our father, Fergus, held the sway
Of his bright shield o'er them as guaranty

Of safety? for none else, it seemeth me,
Shall bring them back. But hear the King again."

"Therefore," the King said, "o'er wide ocean's
plain
Send messengers to Alba's pleasant clime,
And to the Island Fastness; for the time
Hath come at last for Usna's glad return,
And in my heart the fires of longing burn
To see their faces in Ultonian land,
For Friendship's hest hath triumphed, by my hand!"

At once and at his word a mighty shout
Of gladness from the glittering throng burst out,
That stirred the silken banners round the hall,
And, "Who shall bring them back?" cried one
and all.

"I know not," said the King, "for well I wis
That Naisi shuts no eyes upon his bliss;

And he hath sworn with solemn vows no hand
Can lead his footsteps to Ultonian land
Save one of three: Fergus, Roy's kingly son;
And Conal Carna; and our glorious one,
Cuhullin;" and, "Full soon," he muttered low,
"Who loves me and who loves not, I shall know!"
Then brooding from the hall away went he,
And sent for Conal Carna privily.

"Bethink thee, Conal, of the dreadful day
When through Norwegian wilds we took our
way,
Our galley wrecked, and we, two famished men,
Unknowing all, passed by the gray bear's den,
And he rushed out on us with thundering roar
That shook the waste. Upon that desert shore,
Bethink thee, Conal, when the monster's claw
Pierced thy strong shoulder, and his fiery jaw
Opened to crunch thy brass-clad head, how there
With steadfast hand my good sword I did bare,

And in the monster's hot heart made its bed,
And saved thee, Conal Carna! By my head!
Well may I ask thee if thou lovest me;
And if the Usnanians 'neath thy guaranty
Returned to Eman's mansions, and were slain,
What thou wouldst do to him who caused their
bane?"

"But this," said Conal, with his black brows knit:
"The earth and all the hollow caves of it
Should hide him not from death at my right hand,
Who harmed them!"
Then the King: "Like desert sand,
Shifting thy friendship is; and well I wot
That through all change and time thou lov'st me
not!"

Then called he strong Cuhullin. "Ope thine ear,
O comrade! On Beraran's day of fear
Where wert thou, when across the battle wrack

The sanguine sunset flared ?"

"Low on my back,
Within the wood, beneath Beraran's trees,
Upon my laboring breast three foemen's knees,
I lay, O King, and I could almost feel
Touching my throat their brands of bloody steel!"

"Who saved thee then ?"

"None else, O King, but thou
Didst save me! O'er thy helmed and royal brow
I saw the red plume flutter, and I saw
In foam and thunder near and nearer draw
Thy war-steed, with the sharp spur's brazen spines
Rending his gory flanks. As sunlight shines
On Lora's cataract flashed thy valiant blade
Out on the greensward from the bosky shade.
Then all was over. There within the wood
Once more beside thee, King, all-armed I stood;
And there beneath thy sword my captors lay,
Their headless trunks reddening the thirsty clay;

And I was free, and sought the fight again
Beside thee, lord and comrade!"

"Canst thou then
Give life for life? Nay, nay, nay, not thine own!
But should the Usnanian heroes nigh our throne
Come 'neath thy guaranty, what would befall
By thy right hand if death should smite them all?"

"Death and destruction, not alone to thee,
But to thy people all should hap from me,
O King!" the hero said with flashing eye;
"For Trust still lives, and Honor ne'er shall die
Within my heart while life abides therein!"

"Whoso," the King replied, "thy love shall win
Should prize the precious pearl, but I know now
Thou lov'st me not!"

And darkening then his brow
He called for Fergus Royson, and with eyes

Deep searching questioned him full fast:—
"He dies
Who slays them, by this hand, save thee, O King!"

"Thou art their guaranty, and thou shalt bring
The Usnanians back to Eman's mansions bright,
O Fergus! Therefore at the morning light
Spread thy swift sails; but first swear by the
Wind
And the All-powerful Sun, when thou shalt find
Barach beside his house awaiting thee
At thy return, that thou wilt send to me
Without delay Great Usna's sons, that all
May taste their first bread in my banquet-hall!"

And Fergus swore.
To Barach spoke the King:—
"Prepare thy board, O Barach, glittering
With dish of gold and jewelled cups that shine
Of saffron-tinted mead and ruby wine

O'er-filled, and pillage fruitful wood and plain
And wandering stream and ocean's wide-spread
main
For dainty fare, and give at his return
A feast to Fergus, the great knight, forsworn
If he refuse thee; for in gloomy mood
One even he strayed by ocean's tumbling flood
And Daru's house, his father's comrade old
On many a stricken field. With cups of gold
And things of unknown price the board was set
In the gay mansion for the feast, but yet
No pleadings of the old chief could allure
Stern Fergus to the hall. On mead and moor
The morn rose bright, and with it Fergus rose
And sought the place again; but pirate foes
From off the main sea wave had come that night
And sacked the merry mansion, and the light
Now showed his sad eyes where the old chief
lay
Beside his door-post slain! That very day

Before the altar of the Gods, with tears
And sighs of black remorse, 'mid all his peers
Great Fergus vowed to break the law benign
Of Hospitality no more! The wine
Of revel then prepare for him, and there
Feast him as fits a king on dainty fare,
And keep him far from Eman, while I deal
To Usna's sons my feast of blood and steel
And God-sent retribution! Friend, O friend!
Time changes, vengeance never, and the end
That brings my day of reckoning draweth nigh!"

And now as young Dawn up the eastern sky
Walked robed in pink and pearl and violet,
Strong Fergus sought the shore, his white sails
set,
And ploughed the great gray-billow-tumbling sea
Towards Alba's land, and in his company
Took his two sons, stark reapers of the field
Of valor, and the Bearer of his shield,

Huge Collon; and as fast his good ships clave
With brass-bound keels the brine, the spark he gave
His sacrificial fire, and o'er its flame
From the high poop called on the Sea-god's name
With many a prayer for favoring tide and breeze.

Within the wild bright Island of the seas
The Usnanian heroes lived full happily
As moon by moon and year by year went by
In peacefulness. Fair was their dwelling-place.
Amid a lovely wildwood whose green face
Sloped to the sun with all its whispering bowers,
It lay half hidden by the climbing flowers
The ever-changing seasons had given birth
Round wall and fosse. No sounds save love and
mirth
Greeted the listener's ears round that sweet spot,
The cool rill murmuring through the ferny grot,
The ringdove's voice the spiry pines among,
The whisper of the wind-fanned leaves, the song

Of small birds from the grove, the laughter light
Of children dancing on the greensward bright
With pearls of bloom from Summer's golden hand.

Upon a lovely afternoon, when bland
The air was with sweet scents from wood and
plain,
Beneath their trellised home-porch sat the twain,
Naisi and Deirdrè, playing at the chess.
And now no shadow of the old distress
Darkened their looks, for all the memory
Seemed faded of the dreadful days gone by.
From the green wood-skirt came the blithesome
sound
Of Ardan's questing with his hawk and hound;
And nigh them, in his gold-hemmed shining
gear,
Stood Gaier with Ainli casting of the spear,
And shouting as he struck the targe that lay
Across the Green against a tree-bole gray.

"O love!" said Deirdrè, "love! now nought have we
To think of but our own felicity;
For danger from thy conquering arms hath fled,
And joy triumphant reigns, and grief is dead.
Oh! may our lives for ever shine like this,
With no dark cloud to shadow o'er our bliss,
That we may joyful live and joyful die!"
As thus with flushing cheeks and love-bright eye
She spoke, above the green trees from the shore
With long-drawn stress there came a war-horn's roar,
And following soon rang loud throughout the place
The great cry of a mighty man of chase,
That from the distant hills in dreadful tone
Came echoing back. With one hand on the zone
That bound her waist, the other o'er her heart
Pressed close, sat Deirdrè, with her lips apart
And frightened face wherefrom the chilly dew
Of terror fell, as drops when morn is new

Fall from the night-blanched lily: wild she strove
To speak, but only her white lips would move,
And no word came; while eager as the steed
That hears the trumpet call for battle speed
Sat Naisi listening, till the shout again
Filled all the wood. "A mighty man of men,
A man of Erin shouts that shout of pride!"
Glad he exclaimed. "Ah! no, no!" Deirdrè
cried,
With voice at length returning, — "No, no, no!
No man of Erin shouts that shout of woe
To us and ours, — a man of Alba cries
His hunting cry!" Now filling all the skies,
The shout a third time came, and then upstood
Naisi, and called strong Ardan from the wood,
And Ainli from the Green, and, "Go," he said,
Unto the port! Too long have we delayed,
For Fergus calls!"

And Ardan went. "Too well,"
Then Deirdrè cried, "I knew that shout. Our knell

Of doom it is!" Then Naisi: "O delight
Of our strong hearts, why tell not then?"
"Last night
I dreamt a dream," she said. "A pleasant dream
At first it was. Across the ocean stream,
And o'er the gray tops of the Alban hills,
Three bright birds came with honey in their bills
From Eman's mansion to our flower-crowned door,
And lit thereon, and spilled their luscious store
Into the drinking-cups that we held there
Beneath them, feasting on our Alban fare,
That bitter seemed, whenas the taste we knew
Of these soul-snaring drops. Then heaven's calm
blue,
The greenwood spaces, and the sunny plain
Seemed quivering to the sweet melodious strain
They sang of Eman; then away they bore
To Eman back with three red gouts of gore
Dripping from their bright bills!"
"What weird of woe

Read'st thou from this, O Deirdrè?"
"Well we know,"
Said Deirdrè, "than the honey-drops more sweet
The false man's words are when his stealthy feet
In friendly guise approach his enemy;
And the fair words the King will send to thee
By Fergus, though at first full sweet they seem,
Shall end in bloodshed like my hapless dream!"

Meanwhile tall Ardan through the wildwood way
With heart of gladness sought the sounding bay,
And thence did to their sunny homestead bring
Great Fergus Royson and his following.
Then unto Naisi's eyes the silent tear
Of memory rose, and, "O companions dear!"
He cried aloud, "bright blessings rest upon
Your heads from me, the homeless wandering one
Who longs for his returning day by day!"
Then followed greetings glad and laughter gay

And clasp of hands; and while their kind eyes
glowed,
Sweet kisses of fond welcome they bestowed
On Fergus and his sons, and led them in
And feasted them ; and 'mid the joyful din
Asked for the news of Erin.
"News the best,
O friends, I bring; for at the King's behest
I come," said Fergus, "'neath my guaranty
To bear you back to Eman's halls with me,
Where the King's love awaits you!"
"Better far,"
Cried Deirdrè, "here in Alba, where their star
Of fortune, rising, gilds with glorious ray
Their sharp foe-frightening swords, and where their
sway
Shall yet spread wider than your King's, and where
We live a joyful life, unknowing care!"

"Alas! alas!" said Fergus, "on a day
When I was young, I ploughed the salt-sea spray

With venturous keel, 'mid bare Faroean isles;
And there, well practised in the woodman's wiles,
I snared a great sea-eagle in his home
On a wild crag, deep scarred by wind and foam,
And on my galley's deck with brazen chain
Bound him; and with all dainties of the main
Fed him, until my cleaving keel of brass
Cut the swarth sands 'neath high Dunevan's Pass
On Erin's shore. My fortress-gate beside
I placed him, and with kingly pomp and pride
Clasped a gold collar round his neck; but aye
He drooped and pined for his cold rock and gray,
And whistling blasts and tumbling surges' boom.
One morn, when mead and wood with summer's bloom
Were bright, and heaven was bright, I passed him by,
And marked his drooping wing and cheerless eye,
And smit with sudden ruth unclasped his chain,
When up into the blue he soared again

With a fierce cry of gladness, and shot forth
On lightning wing to his beloved north,
And barren crags and ever-booming seas!
So with a man! Though all the braveries
And gold and purple and the smiles of kings,
Yea, all the joys of life this fair earth brings,
Reward him in his exile, what are they,
When, waking from his slumbers day by day,
He sees not — heaven or hell, whate'er it be —
The land belov'd of his nativity?"

Then Naisi: "Well thou sayest; for better still
I love my native land, through good and ill,
Than Alba, though our fortune here is great;
And I will go and bide the hand of Fate
Beneath thy friendly guaranty?"
Whereon,
With troublous eyes and face all wild and wan,
Dierdrè burst forth: "Ah me! ah me! ah me!
Ah! woe, woe, woe! What dreadful destiny

Pursues us?" and she cried and sore besought,
Till Fergus Royson, unto madness wrought,
Swore by the Gods and Elements, the Moon,
The silver Stars, and earth-enlivening Sun,
Should every man of Erin turn his face
Against them, — king or peasant, high or base, —
To harm one hair of their bright heads, no mail,
No sword, no targe, no helmet, should avail
To shield the doer of the deed from death
At his right hand!

Ere blew the morning's breath,
That night, with many a shout and trumpet-blast,
In joy from their Albanian home they passed,
And, as the sunlight gilt the mountains gray,
Gained the bright port wherein their galleys lay.
There, as at swarming-time, Clonmala's bees
With busy murmur crowd the quivering trees,
The great tribe's sailors from the woodland sward
Sprang to the fleet, and crowded mast and yard,

And gave their white sails to the purple morn
And cool, wave-curling breeze; and, outward borne,
Reached the great ocean-swell, and sped away
For Eman; while with face of wild dismay
Sat Dierdrè on the Osprey's poop, her eyes
Turned to the east and ever-brightening skies
And hill-tops that she never more might see,
And whispered her farewell full mournfully:—

"O land of gladness in the orient bright,
No more our feet by dell or daisied height
Shall stray 'neath thy warm suns! No more, no more,
We'll sit by Drayno's music-murmuring shore,
Watching the sea-birds and the glancing ships;
Or where in Masan's vale the wild bee sips
The nectar of innumerable flowers,
With joyous hearts beneath the fragrant bowers
Of sylvan woodbine and delightful may,
Full oft we laughed and sang the livelong day;

No more in Daro's wildwood shall we hear
The cuckoo's welcome note resounding clear
From far-off lapses of blue summer air;
Nor yet by Liath's hill-ridge, free from care,
Feast in the moonlight; nor by Orchay's stream
Cull the rathe blossoms; nor where morning's
 beam
Paints first with gold the pine-tops, shall we see
The youths and maidens in light revelry
Dance at the Beltane time with nimble feet
In Eta's valley, crowned with garlands sweet
As ever bloomed by grove or brooklet strand
Of thy green plains! Farewell! farewell, dear land!"

Then turned she to the westward, weeping sore:
"O home accurst! O dread Ultonian shore,
Why risest thou above the billows bright
To break my heart and blast mine aching sight?
Like a poor bird within the woodman's net
Beating its wings in vain, I strive and fret

'Gainst Fate's stern hand that o'er the wallowing
waves
Steers the long ship that bears us to our graves, —
Alas for my belov'd! and woe is me!"

Now as the next morn's sun full gloriously
Shone on the daisied meads and falling floods
And ferny hills and green Ultonian woods,
The driving keels struck smooth Belfarsad's strand,
And the great tribe in clamor sprung to land,
And with strong Royson's host in loud acclaim
Marched inland, till to Barach's house they came.
And Barach with his ancient face of guile
Came forth and welcomed them with many a smile
And many a kiss of falsehood; and he said,
"Fair is the feast, O Fergus, I have spread
In this my house, and all for thy delight!
And now I charge thee, by thy hand! O knight,
Refuse not, that thy solemn vow remain
Unbroken, from no revel to abstain

Given by a man of thine own high degree!"
And Fergus heard dismayed, and doubtfully
Looked on the sons of Usna, while the glow
Of shame upon his bronzed face seemed to show
Red as the light upon Bengara's crown
In summer when the crimson sun goes down.
"Ill are the words thou sayest, and ill the deed
Thou doest, O Barach, in mine hour of need!"
Stern he replied, "for Usna's sons have sworn
No food to taste, or be it night or morn,
Landing, until they sit the King beside!"
"I charge thee on thy vow," then Barach cried,
"To feast with me!" And Fergus still blood-red
With shame turned unto Naisi, "By thy head!
O Naisi, here this tangled knot thou see'st.
What wouldst thou do with Barach and his feast?"

"Thy choice thou hast to shun the revel gay
In Barach's house, or basely to betray
Thy guaranty!"

"But I betray it not,"
Cried Fergus, "for my brave sons I allot,
Illan and Buinè, unto Eman's hall
To be thy safeguard ; and should, one and all,
The states of Erin rise to work thee ill,
Full strong enough are they to guard thee still!"

"Feast then with Barach," Naisi said, "and we—
We care not. Through the dust-cloud we marched free
Of battle many a day, with nought but these
Our good swords in our hands as guaranties
Of safety, and be sure we fear not now!"

And with fierce eyes and stern contracted brow
He strode away, fast followed by his host
And Fergus' sons. As when on some wild coast,
Barren of home and fruit and all things green,
A wretch is cast, who erst the chief had been

Of a tall ship, and sees his sails again
Spread to the winds by his rebellious men
And the hull sinking o'er the surge; with gaze
Wistful he eyes them through the seaward haze,
And his heart beats with throbs of unknown pain:
So Fergus felt as the long glittering train
Of the two hosts passed on, and from his sight
Was hidden by the ferny mountain height.

As nigh the noontide in a shady place
From their hot speed they rested for a space,
Said Deirdrè, "Husband, hearken unto me,
And turn to strong Dunseverick by the sea
'Neath Conal Carna's ward, and there remain
Till Fergus from the feast come back again,
For well I know with secret sword doth wait
Death for our coming to fair Eman's gate!"
Then Naisi: "Love, what sudden weird is thine?
Once thou didst speak but witching words divine

Of blithesome cheer: now nought for aye will flow
From thy sweet mouth but prophecies of woe!
Be sure no doomful words, no prophecy,
Can turn us from our fate, whate'er it be,
Or good or ill; and we must journey on
Unto the end!"

Then Illan Fergusson
Cried out in anger: "Small the trust, O Queen,
Thou'st gotten in the swords we draw between
Thyself and danger, even though by our side
The sons of Usna stood not glorified
By their high deeds; while our sire's plighted faith
Stands firm to shield thee from all wrong and scathe.
What need'st thou more?"

But she still comfortless
Cried out, lamenting in her sore distress:
"Alas! alas! alas! the day of doom
We left fair Alba and our isle of bloom!
Alas! my heart with grief instinctive breaks,
And bleeds with ceaseless weeping for their sakes,

My well-belov'd. Ah! why did Fergus come
Like a fell blight upon our pleasant home,
With honeyed words our happiness to slay,
And broken faith his victims to betray
Unto the raging King, whose dreadful net
Of wrath and guile for our poor lives is set?—
Alas! alas! the hour that I was born!"

Now from the level fields of waving corn
Again the hosts bright glancing wound, until
They came to Fincarn's watch-tower on the
hill,—
The wild, wind-whistling, far-seen Hill of Foad.
And there as Naisi down the pathway trode
And sought his wife and found her not, aback
He turned along the loud-resounding track,
And saw her weeping by the watch-tower stern,
On the green grass amid the waving fern.
And, "Why delayest thou?" asked he, tenderly.
"A dream," she cried, "O love, that came to me,

While here I slept. Methought with Gaier I stood
Upon a green space all besprent with blood,
And strewn with many a corse; and thou wert
there,
Ainli and Ardan, and the champion fair,
Young Illan, on the bloody sward laid low,
Headless, while Buinè in the level glow
Of the descending sun stood glittering
Safe in his battle harness by the King,
Who looked on us with dread triumphant eye.
Ah! woe is me! our hour of death is nigh.
Woe for brave Illan, and the gentle Three
With whom I traversed many a land and sea
In ceaseless danger, feeling naught but joy!
And woe for thee, my hapless little boy!"

And now unto Ardsalla's height they came,
And Deirdrè with her wondrous eyes aflame,
Like a weird prophetess, cried, "Woe! woe! woe!
O Naisi, see o'er Eman's towers below

Yon cloud terrific hang of crimson stain,
Dripping through lurid air its dreadful rain
Of gore-drops, till all things beneath are red!
O Naisi, stay! Oh, mark this wonder dread,
And flee to strong Dun Dalgan, and abide
Within its lordly halls of power and pride
With brave Cuhullin till the feast is o'er!
Ah, woe is me! yon fearful cloud of gore,
Yon freezing, baleful portent of the air,
I speak and breathe in blood while it hangs
there!
Thou fleest not! Then to Mananan I pray,—
Lord of the crystal-gleaming realm of spray,
Since here no human heart can heed my
moan,
I call on thee! Rise from thine azure throne
Beneath the blue-sky-mirroring, changeful mead
Of ocean limitless, and in my need
Hear thou my call, if e'er in other days
Of joy and dawning love I sang thy praise

To sound of harp and ear-bewitching lute!
Arise, O Mananan, with voice not mute
Of warning, my belov'd ones to restrain
From their destruction! Ah! in vain, in vain,
I call and cry to thee for pitying ruth!
Yet think, — bethink thee of my girlish youth,
My palace fair, my garden all agleam
With many-tinted blooms, my joyous stream
That like a living prayer with melody
Of many songs went murmuring on to thee,
Freighted each morn and evening's dewy hours
By these poor hands with wreaths of votive flowers
For thy delight, Lord of the crystal caves
And pearl-paved mansions 'neath the world of waves!
Then hear my cry, the wailing groans that start
Of agony from out my breaking heart,
And turn my lov'd ones from the dreadful snare!"

Even as she spoke, a breath of gentle air

Blew from the sea-side cliffs and fanned away
The gore-cloud from before her eyes, and gay
The sun shone out o'er plain and willowy height,
And flags and spears and strong battalions bright
Of the two hosts, that now 'gan moving down
At Naisi's word to the King's shining town.
And Deirdrè as she went still weeping prayed,
But no protecting hand her lov'd ones stayed;
And her heart sank within her, till her gaze
Amid the spearmen marked a harness blaze
Upon a mighty Man, who held a spear
In his right hand, bedecked with golden gear
Of rings and studs. A comely face he had,
And wise bright eyes that made the heart feel glad
Where'er they smiled, as he strode stately on
With gait and look familiar, yet unknown.
And as the archers passed, a man went by
Amidst them with a gray, soul-piercing eye,
And belt and quiver filled with many a shaft,
And mighty bow that all with silver laughed

O'er his green-tunicked shoulder; and once more
Amongst the trumpeters a man who bore
A wondrous brazen trumpet in his hand
Adown the pathway strode, as who would stand
Swelling his round red cheeks to blow a blast
Would wake the wide world's dead. Again there passed
With buskined feet, light as the swallow's wing
That skims the green meads in the flowery spring,
Along the way another glorious one,
Amidst the heralds; gay his tabard shone
From twisted torc to tasselled crimson hem
With many a golden thread and glittering gem.
And Deirdrè marked these last as they went by
Look on their lord the Spearman furtively
From time to time with pleasant looks, and said
Unto herself, "Be sure my prayer hath sped,
And all my wailing with kind pity stirs
His heart, who sends in these his messengers,

Or comes himself; for surely this must be,
Yon Spearman bold, the Shaker of the sea!"

Said Deirdrè, as they came to Eman's gate,
"O sons of Usna, heedless of your fate,
List to my words of warning, last of all:
If the King, manful in his own bright hall,
Feast you with Eman's nobles, kind and fair
Your welcome is; but, if he bid you share
The banquet in the Red Branch House, then nought
Can save you from the fell snare he hath wrought,
Save valor and the keen edge of the sword!"

"What boots it now, or cry or warning word?
Come joy or grief, come sweet or bitter bread,
We'll take what fortune sends us!" Naisi said.
And then he bade the trumpet sound. Whereon
Out from the ranks stepped forth that stranger One
With the broad face and ruddy, and on high
Raised his great trumpet toward the sunlit sky,

Puffing his cheeks the while, and blew a call,
Like a wild storm, that shook the ancient wall.
Then forth from out the heralds' place the man
Of the gay tabard and the light foot ran,
And in his grasp the bossy hand-wood took,
And on the door three strokes of thunder strook ;
And, with a loud voice as the clarion clear,
Called through the porch, "The sons of Usna
here !"

THE TRAGEDY OF THE HOUSE OF THE RED BRANCH.

WITHIN his guest-hall did the King arise,
And asked with eager and soul-searching eyes
Where Fergus was. "In Barach's house," they said, —
"The jovial festive-board before them spread, —
He sits with Barach at the revelling!"
Then, filled with secret joy, the crafty King
Asked the feast's servitors how much for food
And wine and mead the Red Branch House was good.
And they replied, "If free from war's stern care,
The Seven Battalions of the land were there

Feasting, twelve moons their revelling might see,
And still of food and drink no dearth could be."
"Then ope for Usna's sons its portals wide,
And spread the board; for broken is their pride,
Their valor a sear leaf before the gust,
Their bright hopes ashes, and their love but dust,
And let them taste the revel while they can,
For sure their life is but a little span!"

When to the Red Branch House now they had
come,
Bright was the board and gay the banquet-room;
For all that one could think or wish was there
Of wine and amber mead and costly fare.
And the King's servitors the dainties plied,
Till all the weary guests were gratified,
Save blue-eyed Deirdrè and the valiant Three,
Who tasted nought, but sat there mournfully,
Brooding and still, aweary of the path
From Barach's house to Eman's hall of wrath.

At last, said Naisi: "If Death tracks our way,
He'll strike the same, or be we sad or gay!"
And the fond twain, for lightening their distress
And dread suspense, 'gan playing at the chess.

Within his guest-hall spoke the King: "No word
Of the false rovers of the sea I've heard,
Nor yet of her, my utter bane and woe!
Now who unto the Red Branch House will go,
And tell me if her beauty lives? For ne'er,
If yet it blooms, did beauty shine so rare
On face and form!"
Then Lavarcam: "O King,
News of the rose and lily I shall bring,
If yet they bloom upon her!" and straightway
Went from the guest-hall, trembling with dismay,
Unto the Red Branch House; and tenderly
Kissed Deirdrè and the well-beloved Three,
And, looking, saw the royal chess-board glow
Between them, with its rich, barbaric show

Of gold-work and of ebony, and said:
"Ill do ye do this perilous hour to spread
The chess-board, that the great King prizeth most,
O children, of all things that he hath lost,
Save Deirdrè's love; and I, even I, have come
At his command, to spy if still the bloom
Live upon Deirdrè's cheek. O red lips rare!
O rose-bright cheeks! O wondrous yellow hair!
O winsome eyes, that soon may look your last!
O matchless one! what witchery hast thou cast
O'er all the world wherever thou dost shine,
That men must worship thee,—a thing divine,—
And fight and die for thee, as in this hall
To-night the valiant Three must fight and fall,
Or conquer for thy sake? To-night, to-night,
O sons of Usna, bitter is your plight,
For you are compassed round by treachery;
And dreadful is the deed the morn shall see,
Wherefrom accurst with everlasting shame
All men in wrath shall hold bright Emán's name!"

Then bade she that they guard their stronghold
well;
And, "Sons of Fergus, be ye fierce and fell
As bears of Orc," she cried, "within their cave
Guarding their young, with valorous swords to save
The Seed of Usna, till your sire's return!"
And with compassion keen her heart did burn,
And from her eyes fell down quick-trickling tears,
As, 'mid the din and lifting of the spears,
Her warning words that answered, she was fain
To seek the guest-hall and the King again.

"Good news and bad have I, O King! The good,
Great Usna's sons across the billowy flood
Have come to thee, and at thine elbow stand,
Conquerors of kings, ready at thy command
To conquer other kings, and make thy sway
Supreme o'er all the isles: the bad, that May
Lends not to Deirdrè's cheek its brilliancy;
For, like a young, light, graceful apple-tree

That in the garden grows, — the slenderest one,
Prinking its satin blossoms in the sun
In all its pride, till with a mighty roar
The storm comes, and the blossoms are no more,—
Beneath Adversity's rough blasts, the rose
No more on Deirdrè's face of sadness blows,
And all departed is her loveliness!"

At this the King's fierce anger and distress
And jealousy abated; and he laughed,
And from his golden cup the red wine quaffed,
And feasted with his nobles, till the thought
Again of Deirdrè to his mind was brought.
Then muttered he, "Perchance one charm re-
mains, —
One charm, enough to set the world in chains
On her bright face; and who will bring me word
More welcome than the tidings I have heard?"
But none he found bravè Usna's sons would spy;
Whereat he, pausing, looked down gloomily,

Stroking his golden-brown beard, mixed with gray,
Then turned to Maini. "Maini, canst thou say
Who slew thy sire and brothers?"
"Well, full well,"
With eyes of fire, cried Maini, "I can tell!
'Twas Naisi, King!"
"Go thou, and tell me true,
If in fair Deirdrè's eyes remain the blue,
And on her cheeks the rose-bloom!"
Maini goes;
And, as he neared the Red Branch and his foes,
His heart misgave him, and the chilly sweat
Of fear and trembling made his swarth brows
wet,
And the frame shrink within his dastard skin;
Even as the churl who doth the hunt begin
Of a brown buck that long had 'scaped his spear,
Within the wildwood by the reedy mere,
And sees his quarry ready for the stroke,
Gleeful, — when nigh him, from some hollow rock,

The selfsame moment rushes in his wrath
A mighty wild beast, growling on his path, —
Trembling he stands, and lets the spear down fall;
So Maini, as he neared the Red Branch wall,
And found the portals barred, with heart adread
Shivered, and thought, "Full doubtful now I tread
Revenge's bloody road 'gainst men like these,
With hearts fulfilled of rage, and memories
Of me not friendly!" Then with stealthy feet,
As the black forest weasel's light and fleet,
He prowled around the Red Branch, till he found
An unshut window full of light and sound
From the great hall, and, peering through, his eye
Marked Deirdrè and her husband silently
Moving the chessmen still, their little son
Beside them laughing. Suddenly as one,
Dreaming of danger, wakes with hurried glance,
And sees the foeman nigh with threatening lance,
Deirdrè, instinctive, laid her chessman down,
And looked and saw the swarth face and the frown

Outside the window, and with secret word
Told Naisi, who a chessman from the board
Took, poised, and threw with swift unerring
aim,
And struck, uprooting Maini's eye of flame
Out of its bleeding orbit! With a yell
Of pain and baffled vengeance Maini fell,
Then rushed unto the guest hall, where all grim
With rage and blood he told what happed to him!

Loud cried the King, "The man who aimed that
cast
Lord of the world might be, should fortune last
And life befriend him for a little space! —
But what, O Maini, of young Deirdrè's face?
And doth her beauty live?"
"O King! O King!
Her beauty is the full June's blossoming
Of all the flowers that in the fair world blow!"
Up sprang the fierce King, a devouring glow

Of fury in his eyes, and knowing not
What his hand held, his jewelled goblet caught
As one would grasp a foeman's throat, and high
Raised it above his head, and with a cry
Of battle anger dashed it on the floor
At Maini's feet; and like the tempest's roar
Called to his troops, who, answering to his shout,
From the great palace portals thundered out,
Swift as the Sea-god's horses raging run
By the bleak Sand Hills and the House of Donn,
What time the Ram shakes in the windy sky
His fleece of woolly clouds, and hail-storms ply
Their wings, wide ocean scourging! Clamorous
In throngs compact they neared the Red Branch House,
With many a shout of vengeance, while within
Of war-cries and of clashing arms the din
No less arose; as when some stormy night
Great troops of wolves adown the frozen height

Rush howling to the hoar Norwegian wood
Where dwell the gray bears and their savage brood;
With yell on yell and hunger-litten eyes
They gird the fastness, while anon replies
The mighty he-bear, with his growl of doom
Shaking the brushwood, and o'erhead the gloom
Is riven by the lightning, and the blast
Tears through the tree-tops! So the tumult vast
Arose and swelled, till backward with a roar
On its great brazen hinges swung the door,
And outward o'er the press rang Naisi's voice:—

"What mean you, men of Eman? Sad your choice
'Twixt honor and dishonor, if you break
The guaranty of Fergus, for whose sake
From Alba's friendly shores our host we bring!"

But they replied, "We serve our lord the King!"
While the King shouted, "By my father's head!
Better that Usna's sons lay with the dead

Than have my wife amongst them!"
Hopelessly
Then Deirdrè beat her breast: "Ah, me! ah, me!
False Fergus he hath brought us to betray!"
But Buinè strode from out the press: "Nay, nay,
O bright one! Be our sire even false to you,
Yet to the guaranty his sons are true,
As thou wilt see with those blue poisonous eyes
That kill all things whereon their splendor lies!"

Then from the house and from the camp behind
He called his troops, and like the sudden wind
That with the autumn thunder in its train
Ploughs up the roaring bay of Beramain,
Forth rushed he furious, and great havoc made,
Till by the King's own voice his hand was stayed:—

"A word! a word, O Buinè, with thy King!
Sheathe thy brave sword; lead off thy following
From this hard field of blows, and Foad's fair land
Of blooming orchard trees thou shalt command,

And many a town beside thou shalt obtain,
And many a fertile tract of ripening grain!"

"What else, O King?"
"Brave Buinè, thou shalt be
My first companion, best belov'd of me!"

"Enough," said Buinè, "To thy hest I yield!"
Then led his fierce troops from the echoing field.

Cried Deirdrè: "Doubly now are we betrayed,
For like the sire the sons!"
Then, as a blade
Drawn sudden from the scabbard sharp and sheen,
Sprang Illan from the throng. "Not all, I ween,
Of the brave race of Fergus basely tread
The path of friend-betrayers!" fierce he said;
"And while this good sword liveth in my hand
Firm to my father's guaranty I stand,
As thou shalt see to-night, O glorious one!"

Then dreadful in his flashing arms he shone,
As he strode forth, and round the house three
    times
Quick circuit made; as on the day of mimes
And feasts and games and jousts on Tailtè's plain,
Around and round competing coursers strain
In the fierce chariot race, and sheer the wind
And champ and foam and toss the dust behind
In rolling clouds, by one great charger led,
Fast rushing on a javelin length ahead
With flying mane; where'er they thundering pass,
Low lie the weeds, the shrubs, the meadow grass:
So Illan from the great door burst, a wrack
Of death and horror strewing in his track,
As through the foe with his strong band he drave
Three times around the Mansion. True and brave
By Naisi was he deemed; for when he came
Back to the Mansion with his eyes aflame
And many a red stain on his battle dress,
There Naisi sat and Ainli at the chess,

Confiding in his guaranty; and when
Their faith he saw, unto his work again
He turned him, like a mower of the mead
By the ale-flagon freshened in his need
Of thirst upon a sultry summer day.
And now to his young son the King did say,
"O Fiachra, on the selfsame hour and morn
Illan and you in this my house were born.
See how his father's panoply doth shine
Upon his stalwart frame! Go, take thou mine,
My two great spears, the Victor and the Cast,
Lightning, my sword, my shield, the Ocean vast,
That on its dazzling orb all work displays
Of the Gods' hands upon the watery ways,
And roars when danger's nigh, till from beyond
High Banba's cliffs her Three great Seas respond
With turmoil furious! Take thou them and go,
And meet fair Illan with good blow for blow!"

And Fiachra in his father's arms arrayed
Went forth and met fair Illan blade to blade

And clanging shield to shield and spear to spear,
And for that each to each was comrade dear
Since childhood, with kind heart pressed unto heart
They first embraced, then moved a rood apart,
And turned, and poised and cast their javelins bright
Each at the other, and with hands of might
Then drew their swords, and on the equal field
Met in mid charge with clash of shield to shield
And sword edge unto sword edge furiously,
Till 'neath the rain of blows upon his knee
Young Fiachra fell, and o'er his crested head
And brass-clad shoulder raised the Ocean dread,
Crouching beneath it. With a mighty sound
That seemed at once from air, from underground,
From rim, from orb, from centre-spike, began
The great shield roaring, till the wrinkled span
Of stormy Cliona answered, and the Sea
Of Rory raised its voice responsively,

Far murmuring, and the furious wave of Toth
Rose round the Giant's Pillars white with froth
And shook its mane loud bellowing!
In a wood
Anigh fair Eman Conal Carna stood,
And heard the voice of Toth; and, "True," he said,
"My King, my comrade, he is sore bested
When Toth gives warning thus!" Then strode away
Through twilight woods and darkening valleys gray
To Eman's Green, where fighting valiantly,
Young Fiachra, brought a third time to his knee,
Held the shield o'er him, Illan with his sword
Upraised to smite. Then strong Dunseverick's lord
Rushed forward blindly, knowing not whose hand
Held high that threatening sword, and drave his brand
Through Illan's back, without the warning cry
That heroes give engaging! Towering high,
Unfallen still, cried Illan:—

"Who is he,
Stealing behind, that striketh secretly
The coward's blow, the sword-stab of the base?
For by my hand of valor! face to face
Fair battle would I give him,—him who now
Hath pierced me through the back."

And who art thou
Thyself?" cried Conal. "Illan Fergusson
Am I, whose blood thou'st spilt, whose day is done!
And art thou Conal Carna?"

"I am he!"
"Dreadful thy deed, for 'neath my guaranty
The Sons of Usna in the Red Branch bide,
And the King seeks to slay them!" Illan cried.
"And thou,—alas for thee, O blind one!" Bright
In Conal's eyes there burned a dreadful light.
And, "By the Gods!" he said, "but vain and small
Is the King's crafty plot where this doth fall!"
And raising his blood-streaming sword again,
He cleft young Fiachra's bright head to the brain

And slew him, and with wrathful strides out-passed
Into the night-black wood!

Now darkening fast
The shades of death on Illan fell. He threw
His sword into the Red Branch House. "To you,
O dear ones, faithful to the last I live,
Now to the Gods my guaranty I give,
And be ye strong and valiant, for no more
Can Illan shield you!" On the field of gore
Clanging he fell, and by young Fiachra lay,
In death not parted!

Now the dreadful fray
Around the Red Branch House and on the Green
Grew louder, for with fires whose blazing sheen
Lightened the lurid heavens, they compassed round
The mighty strong-barred mansion, wall and mound,
Shouting like hunters in some desert glen
Who track the growling wild beast to his den,
And round the place pile up the fagots dry,
And set the flames with many a wary eye,

And upraised weapon ready for the stroke,
Watching the monster maddened by the smoke
Come bursting outward in his savageness;
So wrought they round the House, till through the
press
Broke Ainli with his battle, on the right
His archers, on the left the slingers light,
And in the midst his spearmen; on they came
Whirling the fagots full of smoke and flame
Into their foemen's faces, till at last
They drave them from the Mansion.
Now was past
The third part of the night, when from the door
Of the strong Mansion gleamed the bristling boar
On the great shield of Ardan, as he led
His strong battalions out with tumult dread.
Swift they advanced, innumerous as the flock
Of starlings that beneath Ardfinnan's rock
Seek by the stream bank the rich grasses' seed,
And scurrying onward blacken all the mead.

From wall to wall along the smooth Green's span
A shallow channel with sweet water ran
Before that dreadful night; now black it lay
With blood beneath the flickering torch's ray
And lurid blaze of fagots. 'Cross its bank
Sprang the King's troops, resounding rank on rank,
With hearts of fire the Usnanian charge to meet,
While near and nearer with earth-shaking feet
Rushed Ardan's battle, till in mid career
Met both sides with great shock of sword and spear
And clash of targe and battle-cry: as when
The risen storm tears up Dunvara's glen,
Thrashing the forest with its windy flails,
Incessant, roaring, till it meets and hales
Torc's cataract with fierce stripes, that down its way
Springs, tossing its wild mane of tawny spray,
Fain for the combat; groan and wallowing roar
Re-echo round Killarney's trembling shore

From the dread conflict of the wave above,
The wind below ; so both sides met and strove
With clamor and wild fury, targe to targe,
And knee to knee, till 'cross the streamlet's
marge
Tall Ardan's serried battle forced the foe
And drave them from the Mansion !
Pale the glow
Of the young star of morn now lit the sky,
When round the Mansion rang the battle-cry
Of the King's troops again. Unto his breast
With fond embrace his wife strong Naisi pressed,
And kissed his little son on lips and eyes,
Then threatening in his wrath did he arise,
Made ready by his thigh the Sea-god's brand,
And took his bright spears in his armèd hand,
And poised his flashing shield, and to the lawn
Rushed out far-glittering, like the fiery dawn
That now 'gan rising o'er the hills ; and dread
In wrath he looked, as 'neath Bengara's head

The monster Fiend that meets the affrighted gaze
Of the lone peasant, by the pale moon's rays
Rising from Bala on his seventh year's night,
With eyes like two great beacons blazing bright,
Fell jaws and rough-ridged back and bristling
mane;
Forth comes he clashing loud his loosened chain,
While the belated peasant sick with fear
Drops on the rushy shore as he draws near!
So Naisi rattling in his arms rushed out,
So white with fear the King's troops heard him
shout,
And oft 'gan glancing o'er their shoulders back,
Fain to retreat! The loud-resounding wrack
Of war now covered all the field, the lust
Of blood in fierce eyes blazed, the battle dust
Voluminous arose, and through its shades
Flashed up the standards and the brazen blades
Of spears and brandished swords in the red light
The young morn darted from the eastern height!

Meanwhile within the Mansion Deirdrè sate
In the dark shadow, weeping, desolate,
With no one but the fair Fingalla nigh
And Aoifè and young Gaier; for forth to die,
Or conquer, chiefs and soldiers all were gone,
Save the strange Spearman, whose gilt harness
    shone
With fiery splendor, as he stood anear
Outside the door porch, leaning on his spear
And litten by the full blaze of the sun.
Calmly he watched the surging fight, as one
Untroubled by earth's perils, glancing round
Betimes at Gaier, who o'er the battle ground
Now from a window 'gan to look, and call
Unto his mother.

"Rise thou from the wall
And the dark shadow, mother! Why keep spread
Thy mantle mournful o'er thy drooping head?
Arise, and come to me, and have no fears,
And see the sunlight glitter on the spears,

And all the gallant show and dusty gloom!
Ainli I see, and Ardan! Mother, come,
And hear the trumpets and the bickering
Of sword 'gainst sword, and how the javelins ring
On mail and boss of targe! O strong am I,
By Ainli taught to make the javelin fly
And send the arrow from the twanging bow!
O mother! mother! let me — let me go,
With my bright shining javelin in my hand,
And for one moment by my father stand
And fight for him! Ah! ah! my father! see
Where waves in front the Osprey gallantly!
See how his great sword shears off head and limb!
O mother! was I not born to fight like him?
O mother! mother!" wilder still he cried,
"Give me a sword and place me by his side!
Thou wilt not rise! Alas, art thou afraid?"

Then 'cross the floor he ran, and laid his head
'Gainst her bright head and raised her gently up.

Pale was her cheek as the cold chaliced cup
Of the first pearly snow-drop, as she caught
Her child unto her breast, and fondly brought
His cheek again to hers, and moaned and cried
In bitter anguish: —
"Would that I had died
Far off, far off, and brought thee not to this!
Alas! the dreadful wakening from our bliss!
Alas! death's parting from thee!"
Then the child
Broke from her arms, and, half-bewildered, smiled;
And, "Canst thou fear," he cried, "when on the field
My father shows the Osprey on his shield,
And all the heroes fight the fight for thee?
And here stands one to guard us. Mother, see
How bright he looks and calm! O Spearman bold,"
With wistful look, he cried aloud, "behold!
I pray to thee for that fair jewelled knife
Thou wearest at thy belt; for in the strife

My father fights, and I can strike a blow
Full quick and strong to aid him 'gainst the foe!
Thou wilt not! Ah! why look'st thou so?" for now
There shone a bright light o'er the Spearman's
 brow
And in his eyes; and, lowering his long spear
Beneath the porch, he smiled as he drew near,
And took in his Gaier's outstretched hand.
 "Abide,
O little brave one, by thy mother's side,
And thou wilt see thy father soon!" he said.
Then daintily the strong, bright boy he led
Across the banquet-hall, and placed him there
Beside his mother's knee.
 A trumpet blare
Now shook the Red Branch House, and all the
 Green
Flashed for a moment with the blinding sheen
Of Usna's host, as in their strength and pride
They drove the King's troops back. Then brave
 men died

Beneath their vengeful weapons, numberless
As grass-blades of Glenara's wilderness
In flowery June, or as the wind-blown grain
Of sands on Rossapenna's arid plain,
On a hot morn when drives the summer gust!
And now, from out the rolling clouds of dust,
Victorious, Naisi came, the golden light
Of the fresh morn his strong battalions bright
Illuming, as along their blood-stained track
He led them to the Mansion swiftly back,
And formed their ranks with shield locked unto shield
In a great serried phalanx on the field.
Then loud he called his wife; and at his call
The glittering Spearman strode into the hall,
And led them, wife and eager child and maids,
Into the phalanx of link'd shields and blades,
And took his great targe from his back, and high
Poised it in front of them full warily,

To guard them; while save theirs no mortal ken
Beheld him as he stood!

Now fierce again
The loud-voiced, shrilly trumpets 'gan to sound;
Again the King's troops girt the Usnanians round,
And showers of darts and arrows 'gan to fly;
Again strong Naisi cried his battle-cry,
And Ainli on his left, and Ardan tall
On his right hand, through the spear-bristling wall
Of brass-clad breasts before him thundering drave
With his fierce host, as drives the Barrow's wave
Through the late fields of barley, when the rain
Pours upon Blama's hills, and rock and plain
Bellow with autumn storms! So through the foe
He rushed with his strong host! The gate of woe
They passed but yesterday at length they won,
And slew the guards, and outward in the sun
Burst glittering on the breezy open plain;
And life, with all its loss and all its gain,

Was in their own hands now to bless or ban.
Alas! alas! for over-trusting man!

For now the King to Caffa spoke, and said:
"O thou, whose honeyed tongue might lure the dead
Out from their lonely graves, canst thou not bring
Thy rebel grandsons back to love their King?
For, if restrained not, ruin sure shall fall
From their dread, wrathful hands upon us all.
Then go thou, and with words as Kermad's sweet
Unto my house lead back the wandering feet
Of the three heroes, that fell jealousy
And hate no more may sunder them and me;
And by my father's head, and by the hand
Of a true King and Knight, my faith shall stand
Firm unto them, as stands the Giant's Rock
With high-raised pillared front against the shock
Of Toth's wild wind and ever-bickering wave!"

And Caffa went, believing him, and gave
His hand to Naisi, pledging for the King.
And sweeter than all sounds of streams that sing
Down Banba's sunny woodlands, or the lay
Of birds upon a windless morn of May
From Barna's grove, or voice of breathing flute
In Eman's hall, or love-awakening lute
Played by some fair maid at the silver shrine
Of mild-faced Samain, fell his words divine
Upon their war-worn hearts, as fair he spoke
The false King's message; while a great shout
  broke
Of joy throughout the listening camp; for all
Thought of their homes regained, where Usna's hall
Once gleamed amid its woods by Rory's strand.
And Naisi in his grandsire's placed his hand,
Pledging for his great tribe; and once again
In camp and palace friendship seemed to reign,
And gladness, save in Deirdrè's heart alone.
But she, apart, still made her bitter moan,

Her women round her:—
"O thou land of bliss,
That we should leave thy shores to fall on this!
O Alba of green cliffs and flowery ways,
Farewell to thee and all thy pleasant days!
Once only 'mid thy pleasures did I find
The bitter draught, the poison of the mind
That sears the heart. One day in Camelon,
When round the festive board the wine-cups shone,
And all was gladness and high festival,
In the green rose-garden beside the hall,
I saw my husband meet beneath the bowers
Dunthrone's young daughter, Enna of the Flowers,
The fairest maid of all thy lovely land.
And there he took and kissed her willing hand,
And spoke words that I could not hear. Ah,
me!
The soul-consuming fire of jealousy!
The torments and the wrath! Till Naisi swore
In presence of his arms that evermore

He loved me, — me alone. Alas for him!
How would her young heart bleed, her eyes grow
dim
With bitter floods of falling tears, like mine,
Were she but here to mark the last sun shine
On his beloved head! Ah! desolate,
With me she'd weep their fast-approaching fate,
And we would mingle our sad tears, and cry
Their funeral dirge together, wild and high
And fraught with all our woes; for now their doom
Is on them, and their last dread day is come!"

And now in peace secure the great tribe spent
The morning hours in well-earned merriment,
Quaffing the ruddy wine, the false King's boon,
Till on their wassail smote the beams of noon.
Then, weary with their labors, down they lay
In slumber sweet, and saw no other day;
For from his house the treacherous monarch came,
Out rushing like a fast-destroying flame,

And with his host in sudden fury swept
Over their camp, and slew them as they slept!

Alas! for Love, the slayer of brave men,
Blighter of hearts that ne'er can bloom again;
Oft smiling blissfully in humble homes,
Oft kindling war's dread fires in lordly domes;
Coming in all his glory and his joy
Into the hearts of kings but to destroy,
Envy his handmaid, and his fatal train
Wrath and Despair and Hate and black-browed
Pain,
Revenge with ready dagger raised on high,
Remorse with direful face and downcast eye,
And woeful Murder at the end of all!
Alas! alas! that such a fate should fall
On the beloved Ones whose valiant breasts
Beat ever true and leal. No more their crests
Shall catch the wind of Victory, no more
Their shouts be heard above the conflict's roar

In the brave hours, Time's high-resounding tides,
When the strong hand the fate of hosts decides;
No more with gladsome sound their laugh shall
ring
Round the blithe board in days of revelling;
For now the Three, the flower of Usna's race,
Are captive led to their last trysting place,
And side by side to meet the Headsman's brand
Upon the doomful Green again they stand.

Now as they stood upon that blood-stained ground,
Up spoke the King with all his warriors round:
"Robbers of royal courts! Rebellion's spawn!
At last, at last the fine-spun web is drawn
With fatal mesh around you, and 'tis mine
At last to taste Revenge's fruit divine,
For which I hungered many a weary year,
Even as for her that still my heart holds dear,
The Beautiful, the Bright One, who shall yet
In after days your very names forget,

When you lie rotting underground, and we
Walk o'er your graves in love's felicity!
Now, now you know how far a King's strong hand
Can reach and grasp his foes o'er sea and land,
And drag them surely homeward to his knees,
That he may gloat on their last miseries,
Like me, like me! for this, my day of days,
Hath come at length through long and devious ways,
Purchased by years of thought and steadfast will,
With license manifold and power to kill!
Now, Maini, — now! remember who hath slain
Thy kindred upon Bora's bloody plain,
And bare thy sword, our just revenge to bless,
And send them unto death and nothingness!"

No word they answered, but with steadfast eye
Returned the fierce King's gaze full scornfully.

Said Ainli: "Let me, youngest, die the first,
O Naisi, that mine eyes the sight accurst

Behold not of your deaths!"
Said Ardan: "Nay!
Let me, O Naisi, first explore the way
Unto the gardens of the Gods divine!"

But Naisi cried aloud: "No! brothers mine!
We three shall die together, for my meed
From Mananan will serve us in our need,
This mighty sword that in its scabbard rings
When death is nigh to princes and to kings,
That now even rattles with no gentle shock
Against its iron safeguard. On the block
Stretch we our necks together, and one blow
Shall end alike our gladness and our woe!"

He ceased, and plucked the mighty sword and bright
Out from its sheath, and flashed it in the light
And held it high, and spoke to it: "O friend!
No more to fields of glory thou shalt wend

Beside my hip, to hew the hero's lane,
Hedged round by splintered spears and paved with slain,
Through the thick press of battle; o'er the sea
No more in quest of fame thou'lt sail with me,
And climb the hostile galley's poop, and show
Thy long blade's dreadful splendor to the foe,
Blinding his eyes with terror! — O bright Brand!
Pity that thou should'st touch a coward's hand! —
Come hither, Maini! Tremble not, but take
This foe-destroyer for thy master's sake,
And with it work thy vengeance fierce and fell! —
O world! O son! O wife! farewell, farewell!"

And Maini took the Brand, and silent there
In his strong grasp a moment held it bare,
Then spoke to it: "O glittering gift of price!
O sun-bright boon! O sword of sacrifice!
The Block for my blood-offering, and these
At once the victims and mine enemies,

How have I pleased the Gods that in this hand
I grasp thee for my vengeance, O bright Brand?—
Press close your necks, O heroes!"
Like a flame
Up flashed the sword on high, then down it came,
And cleft the princely white necks at a blow
Resounding on the block!
Ah, deed of woe!

Then at the sight from all that pitying throng
There burst a shout of anguish loud and long,
Three times repeated, rending heaven's bright air;
And with it rose the shrill voice of despair
From Deirdrè, over all sounds rising high
And piercing, like a wounded sea-gull's cry
Heard 'mid the roar of storms, as mad with grief
She ran from side to side, to lord and chief,
Imploring them, not knowing what she said,
Or shrieking in her agony. The dead

Caught her wild eye at last, and down she lay
Beside them, kissing their cold lips of clay,
And speaking unto them in accents low,
As if their dull ears heard her words of woe.
Long lay she, then grew calm and raised her
face,
And called her women to that mournful place,
And said, " O you that followed them and me
From year to pleasant year beyond the sea,
Mark you this bursting heart and tearless eye,
And raise with me their death-song ere I die!"

Then rose the lamentable cry, the wail
Of inarticulate woe that comes when fail
All words the soul's dread anguish to express,
And the heart well-nigh bursts with grief's excess.
And, as it rose, the fierce King's startled ear
Heard 'mid the wail but Deirdrè's voice of fear,
Piercing his bosom like a poisoned knife,
As though with each shrill cry her failing life

Sped forth to follow the brave souls of these
Who now no more could soothe her agonies!

Again distracted ran she to and fro,
Then by her husband's body lay full low,
Embracing, till the blood soaked here and there
The bright gold of her long dishevelled hair.
At length a low, soft Voice fell on her ear,
With gentle soothing sound none else could hear,
And slow she raised her sad face, and behold!
Out through the ranks she saw the burnished
gold
Glitter upon the Spearman's harness sheen,
Where by the far-off ballium of the Green,
He held Gaier's hand, who all unknowing stood
Of her great misery and that deed of blood.
She saw the round-cheeked Trumpeter, and him
Who with light-buskined feet the fields did skim,
Nimble and swift, with his gay tabard on,
And him whose silver quiver dazzling shone

And mighty bow, the Archer, standing there,
And thought, "Ah, now the Sea-god hears my
prayer,
And he will tâke my son unto his home
Where green-hilled Mana smiles o'er ocean's foam,
Far, far away, — ah! far àway from me
And certain death and all this misery!"
She turned, and, as she looked again, her son,
Spearman, and Trumpeter, and all, were gone!
Lowly upon her husband's breast she laid
Her bright head, and great moans of anguish made
That soon grew still.
Then forward stepped the King,
Saying, "Make ready now the sweet harp's string,
Get ready pipe and flute, and open wide
The palace doors for my recovered bride,
Whom I shall teach to curse the name of those
That I have slain, my long-exulting foes!
How pale she looks! but it will pass full soon,
Like a light silver cloud that dulls the moon,

And fades away in one short moment's space
And light returns to her immortal face;
So she will wake and bless my longing gaze!"

Gently he knelt him down, and strove to raise
Her fair head on his arm, but with a pang
Of fear and horror to his feet he sprang,
As limp and cold from out his strong arm's rest
Dropt Deirdrè on her husband's gory breast,
And lay there, never more to rise again,
And live for love, and fight with grief and pain!

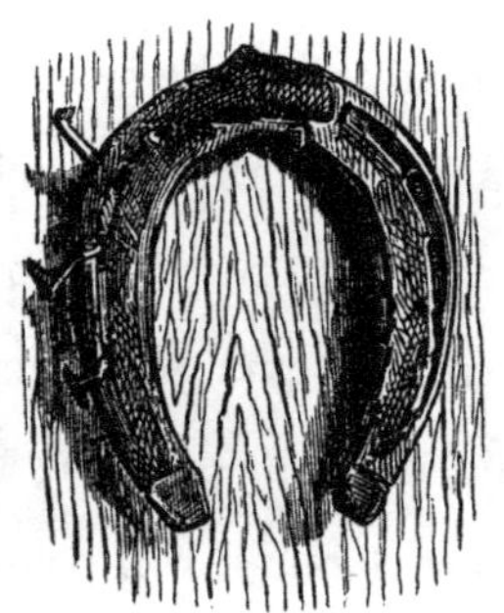

www.ingramcontent.com/pod-product-compliance
Lightning Source LLC
LaVergne TN
LVHW010240110826
845151LV00004B/1350

* 9 7 8 1 4 2 5 5 2 3 8 3 1 *